Malinki of Malawi
Josephine Cunnington Edwards

Pacific Press Publishing Association
Mountain View, California
Omaha, Nebraska   Oshawa, Ontario

Dedication

To Bob and Ruthie Zollinger, and the Laurel-wood school which is more than home to me.

Publisher's Preface

Malinki of Malawi is a true story dealing with life as it was at a certain time in a certain area of the great continent of Africa. Some portions of the book do not make pleasant reading because they realistically portray the people and events that figured in the action.

As one reads the book, he may be impressed with several significant points: (1) Innocent men and women overwhelmed with unwarranted cruelty may still show love and kindness. (2) Men who are in a position to do much good sometimes, when motivated by selfish interests, turn their efforts to evil. (3) Men who operate outside the influence of the Spirit of God may sink to great depths of degradation, but those who respond to the promptings of the Spirit may turn the unlikeliest of backgrounds and the meagerest of resources to the accomplishing of great good.

Where evil is found, let it be abhorred, and where good is recognized, let it be commended. No race, nation, color, or creed has—or ever has had—a monopoly on either of those. In the doing the deeds of men and nations bear witness of the doers.

It has often happened that when the vine grower looked that his vineyard "should bring forth grapes, . . . it brought forth wild grapes." Isaiah 5:2. Just as surely have wild olive branches grafted to tame olive trees partaken "of the root and fatness of the olive tree." Romans 11:17. "If the root be holy, so are the branches." Romans 11:16. The reader should not be surprised to find in this book examples of each kind of human behavior represented by the foregoing symbolism, but he is invited to note particularly how men of any heritage relying on and working with God are able to thwart evil, no matter by whom it is perpetrated, and accomplish great good. Therein lies Malinki's greatest victory and the reason for the publishing of this book.

1

The waters of the mighty Zambezi River in Africa flow onward toward the sea as they have done for millenniums. Raising its furtive eyes above the river's turbid surface in sheltered coves, the stealthy crocodile lies in wait for its prey. So has it done for millenniums. Ponderous elephants lumber down to drink from the shallows by the muddy banks. Wrinkled, gnomelike, black-faced monkeys chitter and peep as they peer through screens of leaves. Great buffaloes, malignant and fierce, crash through the bush, and baboons yap and scamper over the rocks and sun-baked anthills beyond.

Where the Livubwe River flows down into the Zambezi, the little village called Milongo once spread out over the rocks and little rises. The *bwala* in the center of the village, beaten flat almost to iron hardness, had been made by the footsteps of many generations. Here in this little village, Malinki was born more than a hundred years ago to Mwasekera, whose name means Laughing or Happy One.

When Mwasekera was but a small child, she lived in the central part of the country then called Nyasaland at Kadzio village near the rushing Bua River. One year a great drought came upon the land. The time of the beginning of the rains came and went, and the earth became baked and seared. The people gazed in mute appeal at the brazen sky. The drums of the witch doctors beat in vain. Not a cloud drifted across the burning dome. No one planted, for the soil was as dry as the tongue of an old shoe. There was no harvesting, because there had been no planting. Food became scarce, and at last there was no food at all. Wild beasts, crazed with hunger, came into the village and boldly carried off the weaker people. Flesh hung from starved bodies in horrible wrinkled folds. Eyes were sunken wells of hopelessness edged by the gathering scum of disease. Teeth loosened and fell out. Sores oozed; thin bodies wasted away. The people died. Cattle, sheep, and goats lay down by cracked water holes and perished. The Bua River shrank until it became a dirty brownish trickle in some places, and at other places the riverbed lay dry and stony.

Wearing red fezzes on their heads and riding on fat little donkeys, Ajawa traders came one day to the village of Kadzio. And Mwasekera was sold by her own brother to an Ajawa trader. She who had been slim and comely of figure and who had had an unusually pretty face, now gaunt and wizened from the famine, was traded for four quarts of meal!

The traders tied the slaves securely in gangs by the use of slave forks, called *gori* sticks. A long forked stick was placed around the neck of each slave and each stick fastened to another by thongs and chains. Before nightfall the slave caravan left Kadzio village and moved sluggishly southward.

Mwasekera moved mechanically like one in a dream. After several days the caravan reached Fulangkungu Hill, where a thriving village stood. Here the streams had not dried up. There had been rain. Gardens thrived. There was food to eat.

Mwasekera and the other slaves were set to work carrying water for the gardens. Mwasekera, dressed only in a garment made from the skins of animals, bent her young shoulders to carry water all day long from the stream and from the water hole for the crops and for the animals. She was child enough to be comforted somewhat by the abundance of food. But she often wept when she thought of her home in Kadzio village—her mother and father and sisters and brothers. Would she ever see them again?

And then Mwasekera, small, undernourished, and afflicted with rickets, was given in marriage by heathen rites to a man four times her age. Life now became more unbearable for her, made so by the three older wives of her husband.

"Wash this," they commanded, or "Fetch this or that."

"Go do this."

"Sweep here."

"Hoe there."

The commands kept her running from morning till night. She was pinched or hit if she was a little slow or did not please the other wives. At night her legs and body ached. Many times she wept herself to sleep.

As if Mwasekera did not have enough to bear, there

came a greater burden into her young life—motherhood. Not quite fifteen years of age, little "Happy One" bore in misery and wracking pain a sturdy boy child. The old women who watched over her in her labor muttered grimly and wagged their heads knowingly as they clucked: "She surely must die. There must be some evil in her to make her suffer so."

The babe first saw light in the midst of a downpour of cold, tropical rain. Water ran in dirty freshets through the doorway of the mud-walled house. It soaked the mat whereon the slave girl lay, weak and shivering. She named the child Donda, a word contrived from that meaning misery.

The next year a little daughter was born on the same ragged mat. The smell of the unwashed bodies of the women attending Mwasekera and smoke from the fire hole in the center of the room filled the dank, mud-walled hut.

The new babe at birth was placed naked under the unwashed blanket that covered Mwasekera.

Later when she went to fetch water, the babe was tied on her back in a goatskin, while little Donda, her firstborn, toddled naked beside her. When she hoed in the garden, she took both children with her, the one warm against her bare back and the other following close behind her.

As she worked, Mwasekera kept alert watch for the fierce Angoni warriors who were making war on the other tribes continually. Chief Mpenzeni's warriors had devasted hundreds of villages and seized many of the people, their crops, and their animals. Mwasekera knew that when the Angoni warriors came it was as if a fire consumed the countryside. Neither man nor beast nor fowl would be seen for many days after the warriors had passed by. The weak ones of a village—the old, the babes, and the sick ones—were ruthlessly slain.

Stories had been told around the village fires of how women pounding mealies in rough mortars, or grinding grain into flour between two flat stones, or hoeing in the mealie gardens were snatched by the Angoni. As old women were weaving mats or making clay pots, and little children were running here and there in happy abandon, the warriors suddenly came upon them all with blood-curdling shrieks. In an instant all would be fire, turmoil, and death.

2

One morning, while pattering along behind his mother in the mealie garden, Donda seized the corner of the goatskin that held the baby and cried out, "Look! Look! Mother!"

Mwasekera turned quickly. There were the fierce Angoni warriors—dozens of them—painted and decked with feathers and other glittering ornaments, their oiled bodies gleaming like polished ebony. Fear gripped Mwasekera. With a shriek, she seized little Donda and started to run; but she ran into the arms of other painted warriors who came yelling in an almost unbroken phalanx. The babe on her back awakened and began to cry. Mwasekera felt the tiny warm body snatched from her back. She turned to save her babe, only to see her killed. She swung around wildly to snatch up her little Donda, but he was nowhere to be seen.

Once more she was tied in the *gori* stick and chained to others who had been captured. Never again did she see Donda or her husband or the bossy wives.

She had no idea what happened to them. Mwasekera did not grieve for her husband. If he and his other wives were dead or alive, that meant nothing to her. But her heart ached for her cuddly babe and for her little boy. Her back felt cold without the warmth of the tiny body of the little girl. How she yearned for the sight of her little boy, Donda, bending over a pile of dirt or laying sticks one upon another at his play!

The Angoni warriors and their slaves went slowly northward and then eastward. The territory through which they passed was wild in the extreme. Long rows of fires had to be built and kept burning all night to keep away the lions. The very ground seemed to shake with their roaring.

After several days the captors and their captives came to the village of the mighty chief, Mpenzeni. It was a village full of mud-walled, thatch-roofed houses. It swarmed with warriors, curious women, old men, and chattering children. Mwasekera smelled food cooking in pots by every hut. Her stomach ached with the agony of hunger, but she was afraid to speak lest she be beaten.

Once in the village of Mpenzeni, the slaves were separated. Some were sent away to be sold elsewhere. But Mwasekera, wracked with sorrow, hunger, anguish and thirst, waited. She knew not for what. Now that the gori stick had been removed and she was no longer chained, she slipped quietly about, furtively searching the whole caravan and village, hoping to find her little Donda.

Once she ventured to ask the fierce-looking Angoni warrior who had seized her, "My little boy, please, do you know where he is?"

The warrior shouted, "Ho, how am I to know where your little boy is? I am a fierce warrior. I kill many in a single day." He pounded a clenched fist on his well-oiled chest. "How can I remember one small black weasel?"

But Mwasekera remembered and sat speechless, dumb in her agony.

When the tears welled up in her soft brown eyes, the warrior spoke again, "You, girl, you are a fair and pretty one. We will find you a strong Angoni husband. Then you will have more sons. You will quite forget the other who was not worth keeping. You will have many Angoni sons and daughters!"

But Mwasekera shook her head. She was sure that was not true. She felt in her heart that Donda was the most beautiful little boy in all the world, and no one ever had a sweeter baby girl than the child that had been cruelly torn from her back.

Since it was the custom for Angoni warriors to choose one of their captives to marry so as to stamp out the weaker tribe, the day came when Mwasekera was told that arrangements had been made for her marriage to Nzondera, one of the brave warriors.

Mwasekera had seen this man a few times. He was a tall man who carried himself proudly, his muscles rippling under his gleaming skin. "Best of all," Mwasekera thought, "he has no other wives. I will be the principal wife."

When the time came for the wedding, Nzondera brought her seven yards of bright red calico. She trembled from head to toe as she fingered the material and looked at the cloth with wonder in her eyes. She had never owned even a small piece of cloth before in her life. She was sure no one had ever had such a wedding as she would have.

Bulls were killed and barbecued for the wedding feast. Thick *nsima*, made of meal cooked in large pots of water, and pots of rice simmered over the fires. Stalks of sugarcane to be chewed and savored at leisure were brought and laid in piles. Many pots of frothy, bubbly beer had been brewed in preparation for the wedding feast of Nzondera and Mwasekera.

"It is a wonderful feast," Mwasekera declared at the dance, which lasted all night.

So was Mwasekera married to the fierce Angoni warrior, Nzondera. And after the wedding he took her to the village of Milongo, which is on the Livubwe River, which in turn flows into the Zambesi. There Nzondera built a house for his wife and made hoes and other utensils necessary to everyday living. And he and Mwasekera settled down to quiet village life. Days now passed when she did not think of her little ones who were lost to her. And there were times when she even laughed. She worked—hoed, planted, pounded mealies, mudded the floor of her house, and wove mats. Her hands were always busy, and she was not unhappy.

In the course of time, Mwasekera had another son. This one she named Malinki. Looking down into his tiny puckery face, Mwasekera was aware of a great comfort and happiness that came to her.

Nzondera got her a piece of "woman's" cloth (a coarse, sergelike material), which she tied around her waist to carry the little one on her back. Again she felt the warmth of a babe snuggled against her.

Her husband became very gentle in those days, almost as if he had forgotten about warfare. He seemed pleased with the prettiness and youth of Mwasekera. And for his son, Malinki, he showed a great pride.

But the happiness and contentment were short-lived for Mwasekera. One day a brother of Nzondera came to visit. The brother began to berate Nzondera for having taken a slave to be his first wife.

Mwasekera, hearing the loud talk, crept near so she could see and hear what was going on.

"As to having a slave—ho, brother, a slave is well and good for one of your concubines or a third wife. A slave is good for carving, cooking, hoeing, and other such work. I say that is all right. But to have one for your principal wife! Nzondera, are you crazy? Are you a monkey—a lizard?"

"But she is pretty, Chikwiya—" Nzondera said.

Chikwiya spat. "Pretty?" he sneered. "Pretty! What a fool you have fallen to be. Soon you will be telling me that you like her and that little black rat she calls your son. Your blood must be turned to milk, Nzondera. You have taken leave of your senses. Where is your strength and bravery?"

The quarrel went on for a long time. Mwasekera sensed rather than heard her husband weakening, little by little. By the window hole of her little hut she crouched, listening breathlessly and watching every expression on Nzondera's face. After a while, she saw him get up, and without so much as a good-bye to her, he went off down the path with his brother. Her heart became heavy with forebodings.

Mwasekera snatched up Malinki and followed the two furtively for quite a distance. She saw them get into a boat and start across the broad Zambezi River.

Then she returned home to wait.

All that day she waited and hoped against hope that Nzondera would come back to her—would come back to her kindly—with a piece of cloth, a packet of sugar, or maybe a cup. But he did not return.

A few days later one of the village women brought the news that Nzondera and Chikwiya had gone to the Portuguese village called Tete on the other side of the big river, and they were going to Mpenzeni. "They told my husband that the chief will make another war soon." She paused and wrung her hands. Then she went on, "These wars! Oh, these wars! Will they never stop? We bear many men-children only to see them killed or sold."

Mwasekera never saw her husband Nzondera again, and soon Malinki would have no memory of him. But Mwasekera treasured many bright memories, for was he not the father of her little Malinki? And had he not always been a kind husband? And had he not brought many gifts to her?

She never knew whether he had died in battle or in a drunken fight, or had been eaten by wild beasts —or whether his life had been ravaged by dysentery or malaria.

What she did find out was that she had been sold once more as a slave. She and her little one, Malinki, had been sold to an Ajawa trader. The trader, named Chikunda, came to Milongo village and showed significant papers to the headman. They were to the effect that a certain Angoni warrior named Nzondera had gone through Tete and had sold a certain woman named Mwasekera and her babe for a gun, some bullets, a length of cloth, and a jug of Portugese rum.

2—M.O.M.

And that was all. Mwasekera and Malinki had been sold.

One look at Chikunda, the Ajawa trader, a gigantic man with rippling muscles showing from under the blanket that hung negligently from his shoulder, showed that he was a ruthless man, full of evil and avarice. When he spoke, his voice sounded like that of a bellowing bull. Always he had his *chikoti* with him, the rhino whip which could cut a man's or woman's back into ribbons, and Chikunda seemed always ready to use it. This man would stop at nothing to gain his desires, it was reported. The use of fiery Portuguese rum did not improve his villainous temper.

A vast tract of land was in Chikunda's possession, and slavers constantly came to him to barter in human lives. He chose and changed wives at will, so a cluster of huts around his own buzzed with women's activities. The thump of the grinder grinding mealies into flour for the making of the thick mush called *nsima* that he loved was heard almost constantly as his wives worked to satisfy his appetite. He had cattle, hundreds of them, grazing under the watchful eyes of slave herders. Cattle meant riches. They could buy a woman if he chose to buy rather than take. His slaves feared and loathed him.

For such a man Mwasekera took up the hoe to cultivate his garden. Her job was also to fetch water and help in the pounding of the mealies into flour. She worked from morning till night day after day. Always it was for someone else that she worked and slaved. For herself and the other slaves the most miserable food was allotted, until in weakness and desperation they stole whatever they could get. But Mwasekera

18

and the others were convinced that it was not wrong to take from one who had so much. The wrong became apparent only when they were caught and severely punished.

One day Chikunda told Mwasekera that a husband had been chosen for her. This time there was no wedding feast. She simply took her babe Malinki and went to stay in the hut of Kwanona, another slave of the evil Chikunda.

Mwasekera's eyes brightened a bit when she saw the hut, set off to one side of the village. To her it seemed just a little better than the other huts. She had no possessions, no dowry, nothing to carry with her save the baby Malinki, who in time, proved to be greater riches than any dowry to both of them. But who could tell that on the wedding day?

Kwanona stood at the door of the hut to meet her. He was a tall man too, but gaunt from starvation. Raised irregular welts covered his back. These were scars made by the lash of the *chikoti*.

Kwanona must be a very strong man, Mwasekera thought as she entered his hut. But surely he had known much suffering and anguish.

Strangely enough, Kwanona treated Mwasekera with kindness and tenderness. His voice was soft and gentle whenever he spoke to her or to the babe. He, too, had suffered greatly in his years of servitude, and he was a man of leadership and spirit, one who could not face slavery with submission or grace. Hence, the scarred back. Tears streamed down Mwasekera's cheeks as Kwanona told her how his first wife and children had been cruelly separated from him in one of the wars of Mpenzeni. Kwanona had fought valiantly for his liberty at that time but against hopeless odds. He told how he had seen his old mother clubbed to death, and his babe brained against the trunk of a tree. Mwasekera knew well how he felt. Had not her babe been torn from her, and her small son also?

That night when Mwasekera and Malinki moved into his hut, Kwanona crept out and, at the peril of flogging, stole one of Chikunda's chickens. Then he and Mwasekera in a little inner room gleefully cooked their chicken and some nsima over a tiny fire. That was their wedding feast. They smacked their lips at the taste of the fowl. "Like the dew of the morning," Kwanona said, as they sat there and ate every bite. He then dug a hole in one corner of the hut and carefully buried the chicken feathers and bones, lest their action be discovered and they be beaten.

When they were ready to sleep, Kwanona rummaged up under the grass of the eaves of the roof, and finally brought forth a great blanket, dank, heavy, and dirty. "This, too, I stole!" he chuckled gleefully to Mwasekera as he spread it out on the mats. "But I do not care, for they stole me, didn't they? They have no right to me or to the work I am forced to do, so I steal. And I will steal until my belly is full of their riches." He rubbed his stomach and grinned. "And one day, when I can plan with great care, and when the country is a little more peaceful, we will run away from this fellow and find freedom. This boy," he laid his hand on little sleeping Malinki, "will not be raised in slavery."

That night tiny Malinki slept under a piece of harsh bark cloth his mother had peeled from the momba tree and pounded to resiliency for his blanket, his small mind and belly at ease. Then Mwasekera and Kwanona wrapped in their stolen blanket, slept until the morning brought again its train of burdens, labors, cursings, and privations. But both of them went into the next day's work cheerfully—almost gaily—knowing that when evening came there would be a fire, a blanket, some food, and love and sympathy for each other.

Every stroke of the hoe in the days that followed seemed to bring Mwasekera closer to Kwanona and filled her with laughter and love. Tiny Malinki called him father immediately and ran down the rocky path to meet him when he would come home late calling, *"Bambo! Bambo!"*

And so Mwasekera and Kwanona began a sort of married life together! It was a queer, harried, unofficial married life in which neither church nor tribe had any part. Chikunda himself was the master, Chikunda the Terrible, with no mercy or sympathy for those whom he held in his wicked clutches.

Mwasekera knew that Chikunda would not sell Kwanona. In her simple mind she knew that things could never be worse. Kwanona was too strong, too valuable to be parted with. He made Chikunda richer every day, even though he did so unwillingly.

One day Kwanona was ordered to help kill and butcher an ox. He left Mwasekera and Malinki and went with the other slaves to kill, skin, and cut up the animal. Mwasekera and Malinki went to the garden area to hoe soon after Kwanona left them.

That was a terrible day. Suddenly Mwasekera stopped her hoeing. She heard screams and the stroke of the dreaded *chikota*. Little Malinki ran and threw his arms around her legs and cried. She pressed the child to her, and her heart raced with fear and premonition.

"Maiye! "Maiye! "Maiye!" she heard the screams over and over, for that was the lake people's cry of sorrow or pain. Beatings were frequent, so she dumbly began to hoe on, hardly realizing her own misery and foreboding. But Malinki would not leave her. He clung to her legs and whimpered pitifully. How could she know that the beaten one was Kwanona, her beloved Kwanona the good? Even if she had known, for sure, even then there was little or nothing she could do about it but suffer and agonize.

Presently, the babble of voices came nearer and yet nearer. She left her hoe, and crept up the hill, fearful of what the hullabaloo could mean. On a rough machila carried by the slaves lay an unconscious form. As she crept nearer she saw it was her husband, Kwanona. Bloody ribbons of flesh, turning black and stiff, hung from his back. As he groaned, spittle ran from the sides of his mouth. The dirt on his face was furrowed by tears.

Then Mwasekera began to wail too, in the characteristic way of the poor African mourner; for surely Kwanona, the kind one, was dead. *"Maiye! "Maiye! Cisoni ndithu!"* she shrieked, beating her chest in agony of grief. *"Maiye! "Maiye! "* and little Malinki seized one of her legs and buried his tiny face in the goatskin that hung from her waist and joined his small voice to her screams.

"Hush! Be still," one of the women called out. "Kwanona is not dead, but he will be if you tear off his very ears with the noises you are making. Hurry now and make haste with hot water and medicine."

They carried her husband into the small hut and laid him face down on the mat she hastily unrolled. Already he was gaining consciousness and groaning heavily. Mwasekera, tears streaming down her cheeks, tried to bathe and care for Kwanona's horrible wounds. She worked over him as well as she could, with the primitive remedies she had at her hand, crying all the time from fear and dread. Supposing Kwanona would die? What would *she* do?

Presently, he opened his eyes. "Mwasekera," he whispered, weakly.

"Yes, Kwanona—" she knelt beside him as he made feeble, fumbling movements toward the harsh piece of cloth folded roughly about his hips, one corner pulled up between his legs. "Look—look—there inside, there between my knees, quickly, while no one can see you."

Puzzled, the girl leaned over and patted around on the rough loin cloth. Inside, between his knees, she discovered a huge lump of something. Still more puzzled, she loosened the folds, and reached in and drew out a huge, wet chunk of lean meat. Quickly she looked at Kwanona's face. A wan, crafty smile had crept up over the pain-pinched features.

"He beat me for taking it for you, my beautiful one," he whispered weakly. "He took it from me. Then when they picked me up, they thought I was sleeping with the pain, but I got it again. Go, cook it, Mwasekera, but make the fire small. I could drink some broth, I think. You and the boy can feast."

"Oh, Kwanona," sobbed the girl. "Do not steal for me! It kills me to see you hurt so badly. It is better never

23

to taste such food than for you to die and leave me alone. For you are all I have to care for me."

"But it is not stealing," he protested in a loud whisper. "It is ours if we can get it, for he has no right to keep us. I will escape from this devil. You will see— and soon—soon. Or else, I will kill him. I will not take this evil much longer."

"Oh, don't talk so," the girl begged. "Oh, Kwanona, what will be the end? Will we die in this slavery? Isn't there anything for us? Why were we born? Why do we live when life is only a load to be carried with pain?"

"Go cook the meat, girl. Some good lean meat will comfort us both, and make Malinki's stomach stick out like a clay pot." He groaned as he tried to turn on the mat to ease his throbbing wounds.

Mwasekera went to cook the great chunk of meat over a small fire. While it was cooking, she crept out to find some soft, healing leaves to pound into a moist pulp to make a poultice for Kwanona's lacerated back. By the time the poultice was ready savory odors, tantalizingly delightful, filled the hut. Mwasekera, holding a little clay bowl, knelt by Kwanona's side and gave him broth to drink. He gulped it eagerly, sighing a little after every swallow.

Darkness had fallen over Chikunda's village—a sullen, throbbing, darkness, full of menace and hatred. Soon someone rattled the rough bamboo door mat covering the *khomo* or door hole of Kwanana's and Mwasekera's hut.

"*Odi!*" [We are here] someone whispered, asking admittance. "*Odi, odi.*"

"*Odini!*" whispered Mwasekera, rolling back the mat a little fearfully.

A fellow slave glancing over his shoulder fearfully stood in the half light offering Mwasekera something wrapped in a banana leaf. "For Kwanona," the slave whispered. "The cook of Chikunda sent this food secretly, for there is fish for Chikunda tonight. We are all sorry for what happened. We will kill Chikunda someday. You will see." He vanished into the darkness.

There was some comfort in what he said. Mwasekera unwrapped the fish and began to separate the crispy pieces, giving some to little Malinki. Then she knelt to put some bits of tender, flaky fish into Kwanona's mouth.

Just then the matting rattled again.

"Odi!" another voice said. "Odi, odi!"

This time one of Chikunda's slaves brought a pot of rice, filched also from Chikunda's bountiful store. It had been dropped slowly into boiling water, covered, and simmered until it was tender and puffy. Mwasekera shook her head as she brought it in. Kwanona was a man well-liked, that was certain. Soon another came, bringing bananas, and one brought sweet potatoes roasted in hot ashes. One brought a clay bottle of liquor made from bananas and palm fruit. It was as strong as whiskey and potent as fire. Kwanona drained the clay bottle of all its fiery contents. In a little while he was unconscious of his misery. But for the next few days he could not even rise from his mat, much less work. He lay on the mat in great pain, his back a fiery furnace of angry, throbbing sores, now oozing pus and blood. But Mwasekera knew of many succulent weeds and leaves which she gathered. Pulverized and made into a paste, these could make Kwanona's pain a little less. Kwanona sighed as he told her it was delightful to just lie still and rest. Now he did not mind his wounds so much.

But long before he was able, Kwanona was driven back to his work. He was used to agony. He had lived with it for a long, long time. It seemed to be the only heritage he would ever have.

So, slowly, all too slowly, time passed by—a kaleidoscope of harshness, suffering, and misery. One, two, three, four more years of slavery went by. Kwanona's determination to escape grew, but he knew he must plan carefully.

With the innate patience of the primitive Africans, Kwanona and his brother Kandiado laid stealthy plans for escape. Both men determined to get away with their families, even if they all died in the attempt. They kept this plan secret from all the other slaves. And they determined not to die. Day by day, a pinch of this, or a handful of that, or a bit of something else was stolen from field or store. Rice, beans, meal, biltong, dried peas, all found their way into skin bags and were hidden away carefully. Little by little their supplies grew.

The hour finally came when Kwanona decided they were ready to go. They had all they dared to carry. They would go in the middle of the night. On that night, dark and cloudy, without benefit of moonlight they stole forth quietly, fearfully. The wrath of Chikunda, they well knew, was no better but was even worse than the lion or leopard who terrorized whole villages and killed great bulls and cattle for food. Their fate would be worse than death if Chikunda caught them trying to escape. But even so, death would be sweeter than this life they now lived.

3

And so the ragged, tattered little group went forth silently and furtively, Mwasekera with her new babe, a girl whom they had named Linnesi, and Malinki and Kwanona along with Kandiado and his wife Gafiyodi. Gafiyodi and Kandiado left behind them the graves of their two little ones who had died in infancy. The group hardly dared breathe until they saw behind them the village shrouded in a thick mist. Then, a kind of subdued gaiety possessed them. Weary, aching legs stepped more briskly. Heads, so long bobbing on weary necks, were lifted to a brighter horizon.

Were there crouching wild animals to fear on the journey? What about poison snakes hanging in trees, or slithering through the tall grasses? Certainly they were there to be wary of, yet the little group gladly braved the perils of the forest and the bush for the delicious sense of freedom, freedom which they tasted so seldom and which could be so soon snatched away. Tirelessly they put miles behind them, going as swiftly and as silently as they could. Hardly a bush swished, or a twig snapped, so carefully did they tread along the path. Even the children tried to be quiet. Mwasekera reached back to pat the small child snuggled on her back in a smooth warm goatskin. She had been born to Mwasekera and Kwanona back in Chikunda's village a month or so before. Her birth had never been recorded. What difference did it make? It didn't change things for slaves, whose toil and lives and destiny belonged to someone else.

Kandiado, the brother of Kwanona, carried little Malinki on his strong shoulders. The two women and Kwanona carried food and the weapons. It had all been arranged beforehand. Before the morning of that escape night had dawned, many miles lay between the little group and their evil master, Chikunda. For the most part they followed paths made by animals. Elephant grass towered eight and ten feet high on either side, leaning over to form a green tunnel through which the group crept. The grasses lashed wetness in their faces, and even though their feet were as hard as leather, the stones and the briars were cruel. Little stinging insects followed them in swarms.

Even though they were tired, they dared not stop. They crept along all day, weary now to the point of weeping, but they dared not halt. They were inured to endurance and suffering. When the children began to cry in soft little whimpers, a harsh "Cete!" hushed them. The sun slanted toward the west, throwing reddish shadows across the tangled bush, when at long last they dared to stop. A tiny babbling stream flowing merrily over the stone attracted them.

"Husband, let us stop here," pleaded Mwasekera.

"My feet—they are as if fierce fires are burning the blisters and my throat is dry. The little ones are tired and hungry."

"I, also, am ready to fall down like a dead bird," said Gafiyodi, the wife of Kandiado. "Let us rest here. No one will find us now! We are very far, I am sure, from that Chikunda."

"We must build fires to scare away the lions and the leopards and the wild pigs," Kwanona said.

So they all helped to gather wood—great heaps of it—to keep fires burning during the night. Soon Kwanona had a great fire leaping toward the sky. Little Malinki ran here and there, gathering small twigs and throwing them into the roaring fire. His eyes shone as he tossed them into the fire and jumped up and down clapping his hands.

Gafiyodi began to cook the meal of nsima, while in a smaller pot she had dried fish stewing for a relish in which to dip little balls of the porridge.

"Come, Malinki," called Mwasekera, laughter in her young voice. "Let us go and wash in the little stream. It will put new life into our legs and bones!"

Malinki, naked as a very young bird, ran after his mother. She plunged the baby, Linnesi, into the cool shallows until the little one shrieked with fear.

Gafiyodi caught the spirit of gaiety and pulling the pots of nsima and fish from the coals, she, too, flung off her goatskin and plunged into the water. Soon Kwanona and Kandiado were with them, all enjoying the cool water with the freedom of little children. It soaked into their sweaty, weary bodies and gave them all renewed energy. They played and frolicked like children in the cool freshness of the swift flowing water. Before the sun had quite "gone to sleep" they all came up to eat. They rolled the *nsima* into little balls, dipped them into the salty fish relish, and then popped them into their mouths. After the meal they scraped places clear of grass, for biting ticks hid in the grass. Their bite would cause much fever and sickness. In the cleared spot the weary travelers could lie down near the fire to rest. Already Malinki, relaxed and free from troubles, lay asleep, his tiny finger in his mouth.

Tired as they were, Kwanona and Kandiado took turns at sleeping that night. They had to keep the fires going to keep away the leopards and the lions. Even so, the great beasts crept as near as they dared, and their coughing and roaring occasionally awakened the little ones and set them to crying. But a pat from the mother's hand or a word of assurance quieted them again.

At dawn Kwanona went off to hunt. He killed a wild pig to bring to the still sleeping group and brought back also a goatskin full of yellowish berries he had found growing by the edge of the water. He squatted by the fire roasting the pig. Savory odors of the browning flesh began to drag the others out of their sleep.

"All of you wake up," Kwanona shouted. "We are free! Free! This day we do not fetch or carry or hoe or run at the beck and call of Chikunda, the wicked. And here is food! Food! Food for all!"

In the midst of the rush for browning chunks of roasted meat, Kandiado appeared. He, too, had gone on an early morning hunt. He had a young buck slung over his shoulders. A great shout arose from those around the fire. Even with the grease of the wild pig plastered all over their faces, they savored the idea of more meat. They had not known such luxury or variety in all their lives. The women cut the venison in strips and dried some of it, making biltong as some of the tribes called the dried salt meat. They would not have time to fix much to take with them, they well knew. The meat of both the wild pig and the buck had to be cooked. The morning was half gone before they got started on the second day of their journey to freedom. Loaded as they were, they started off in buoyant spirits. They were free, free to live out their simple lives themselves with no interference.

The journey that the pitiful little group made from Milongo village to Chikwawa in Kasisiland would seem every insignificant today. Nyasaland, poor, barbarous, slave-ridden, war-scourged Nyasaland, stood on the brink of greater things. The morning sky reddened for a brighter day. Little Malinki would not have to suffer as his mother or his stepfather had. He would work, but he would not be so oppressed. These poor ones creeping fearfully through the unbroken bush knew they had much to fear. There were warring chiefs even yet who were willing to catch and sell them for such precious possessions as guns, cloth, dishes, or rum. Arab and Portuguese traders were everywhere on the lookout for "black ivory" to chain and march in miserable gangs to the teeming slave market at Zanzibar, hundreds of miles to the northeast. Thousands were caught and sold every year. No one was safe.

The rivers were full of crocodiles, one snap of whose jaws could sever a limb or cut a child in two. Lions, leopards, and hyenas were abundant, to say nothing

31

of the cobra and the mamba. The greatest killer of all was malaria, although at that time no one was certain of the cause of the dreaded fever. It was a battle to live against the terrible odds of the Dark Continent.

The very year of the group's escape from the servitude of Chikunda, David Livingstone was working up and down the mighty Zambezi River. Three times before Mwasekera had left Milongo, the missionary-explorer had been in Tete, only a few miles down the Livubwe River from where they were. Rumors had come to them there that certain creatures had come up out of the sea—queer white creatures related to fish. The people talked and conjectured about them at great length. No one seemed to know anything for sure. One man who had seen David Livingstone while he was at Tete had walked all the way to Milongo with the amazing, unbelievable story that the white man's bowels were on the outside of his body. Presumably Livingstone had worn a necktie, and when the people saw it moving slightly when he ate food or drank water, they immediately believed it to be connected in some way with the digestive system. The whole village questioned at length the one who had seen Dr. Livingstone, wondering if the creature was a man or a beast.

That year, 1861, saw many world-shaking events. Even Africa felt the imperceptible changes creeping in which would color and change the whole philosophy of life. Chief Lobengula gathered power. Paul Kruger was planning to outwit Lobengula. Far across the ocean in the United States a war between the North and the South had begun. A civil war against slavery was being fought.

But of these events Mwasekera, Kwanona, and the others with them were ignorant. Now there were many days of travel and nights of vigilance and anxiety. Once they spied a party of Arab slavers far across the bush. Before they could slink to safety, a young doe, trembling and terrified, sprang out of the grasses and ran swiftly down the steep hillside. The Arabs were after it instantly, savoring, no doubt, fresh meat for themselves. Only by that slender circumstance was the little group saved from discovery and recapture. The fugitives hid for two days after that, hardly daring to move abroad.

At long last the little party reached a rich valley near the Mwanza River in Kasisiland. Kwanona's discerning eyes saw the fertile spot first of all. It lay there as if it were waiting for them. There was land, trees, and water, and an abundance of game. "Onani, Kandiado!" he cried out excitedly—in this way calling his brother to look. Both threw their loads on the ground and feasted their eyes upon the scene. Instantly the men were down on their knees examining the rich soil. Trees, enough for firewood for a long time, grew nearby. The land was level, sloping only slightly down to the banks of the Mwanza.

The bush formed a crescent there. It was a perfect place to build their simple huts and raise the food necessary for their existence. The women had brought seeds among the things they had filched from evil Chikunda.

"This place is good for hunting too," Kandiado remarked, looking about at the sweep of hills surrounding them.

It was late September—the dry season in central

3—M.O.M.

Africa—and very hot. Little rain had fallen since the preceding May, and most of the stream beds stretched out crooked and dry. Even the Mwanza had gone down until it was a very small trickle meandering about in the center of the dry, rocky riverbed. But in the rainy season Kwanona knew the water would flow, cool and abundant.

Even while these freedom-starved people were building their crude mud huts, lugging water up from the river to mix with earth, David Livingstone and Dr. John Kirk were struggling through dense growth to see for the first time the broad, shimmering expanse of Lake Nyasa. David Livingstone would bring the good news to the people of that land.

After the houses were built, they were roofed with the long grasses cut from the bush. Kandiado and Kwanona then took the seeds which had been filched from Chikunda and carefully prepared and planted a garden near the stream, where it could be watered easily and kept growing. No rain could be expected before mid-November. Corn and pumpkins and garlic were planted. Beans were planted too so that they could climb up the corn stalks and hang in bunches to be easily picked.

The task of keeping the monkeys and baboons out of the precious garden became Malinki's job. Although only ten or eleven years old, he helped to build crude fences around the garden and pit traps at intervals to protect it from the nightly visits of the wild pigs. He sensed that they must all fight their enemies or there would be no food. A dead crow hanging from a branch would usually scare away crows for a while. Later, Kwanona built a tall shelter in the midst of the field as a baboon lookout. Everyone took turns watching and making noises in the high shelter to protect the crops from the baboons, who could riddle a field in a couple hours.

After they were settled, Kandiado and Kwanona prepared to go to Kasisi to pay their respects to the chief who ruled over that vast area. They would take with them salt that the women had made by boiling down some of the salty soil and laboriously extracting the precious mineral salt. A small rough bag of this was prepared as a present for Apito, the king, and another bag, to use in trade for some chickens, if any could be found. Another small bag was prepared with which to buy other things. Everyone helped in the preparations for the journey. Corn and sweet potatoes were roasted to take along for food. A little bag of biltong would serve a good purpose too.

When Kwanona and Kandiado left, the women well knew that they might never see their husbands again, for those were days of real danger on every hand. A man might go for a day of hunting to return and find his whole village pillaged and burned. Everyone would be gone, save the dead, who could tell him nothing of what had occurred. Or a man might go to the stream to take a bath or go out to hunt and never return. How eagerly and fearfully then did the women and the little ones await the return of their men. Harassed by this devastating business of slave trade, this part of the lake country was sparsely settled. One could walk thirty, even forty miles and never see a village. True, there were blackened ruins—places where once populous villages had flourished—but the bush soon took over and obliterated all traces of human habitation until one would have thought the clock of time had moved back to the early days of the world, so quiet was it, so lonely and so still.

While the men were away, the two women and the children slept in one house for company and safety. They knew that it would be many days and nights before their husbands could possibly return to them.

Many days later Malinki was set to watch and herald the return of the loved ones when they would appear. Would they return home, or would their journey's end be in the slave market of Zanzibar or in the stomach of a wild beast? Such were the perils of those days.

At last the two men returned, footsore and weary, but safe. Malinki shouted to his mother and Gafiyodi, who ran out with shouts of joy to greet their husbands. How the little group chattered, everyone talking at once as they returned to their huts.

"Moni, Bambo!" Malinki reached shyly for the hand of the man who had been a good father to him. His eyes glowed as he looked up into Kwanona's face.

Little Lennesi held up her tiny hands and squealed with joy, remembering her father.

They all went to the stream nearby to wash. After they had eaten, there was still enough daylight so they could examine the things the salt had bought. The men showed their goods to Mwasekera and Gafiyodi; six hens and a rooster in a rough bamboo cage Kandiado had fashioned and tied with luzi (bark string). The king, Apito, had given each man a piece of red calico as a gift for the salt he had received. The salt had been the whitest salt he had seen, Kwanona told the women.

The women touched the cloth over and over again, expressing joy over possessing such lovely material.

In the skin bags the men had brought home dried peas, cassava roots, millet, and some rice. A little could be eaten, but most of it had to be saved for seed. Soon the heavy rains would fall, and they must plant a big garden. Then there would be plenty of everything for all of them and some to spare, which they would sell. After rejoicing over the trades, the women released the chickens, squawking, weary wild things which would later sleep in houses for safety from hyenas and leopards. After the two women had built a big fire, they all sat around it while the men told of meeting with Apito, the ruler of Kasisiland. Kandiado, being more talkative than Kwanona, told the story while Kwanona nodded and said from time to time "ndithu" (certainly that is true).

"You children, all, just listen to me," Kandiado counseled the group sitting around him. "Whenever you go to meet some big man, or some great one, you must never stand up high over him so your head is higher than his head. Oh, that is bad manners, *kwabasi* (very much). When you go, you must stoop as low as you can, so you are lower than he is. That's the way you show him you think he is a big man and you can't possibly be as great as he is. Then, before you ever go near, the guards call out, '*Bayete, 'n kos! Bayete, 'n kos!*' You don't move till you get the answer." He paused and looked around at his audience. "Then it is good," Kandiado resumed, "to keep clapping your hands softly, and smiling, for that shows you salute him as a king. It is bad manners to go behind the king's back. Always pass in front of him. In the olden days enemies slipped behind the king's back, and sometimes the king was killed by an enemy who slipped behind him."

Kandiado stopped talking to peel a little length of sugarcane with his teeth. By now night had dropped her curtain all about the little group. Even the rosy glow of the very short twilight was gone. Somewhere not far away a hyena screamed out in its hideous half-laughing, half-crying way. But the hyena did not frighten those gathered about Kandiado. They knew it was a coward.

"Do not ever forget," Kandiado started to speak again, "always hold out both hands when you receive a gift. If you hold out only one hand, you will be despised and beaten by the big men, and the gift will be taken away. That is not good manners, and it is time you learned manners, for we are not slaves anymore."

Now Kwanona spoke up. "That is the way we met Apito, and he was very happy and kind to us. After he had received our salt, he said it was the whitest he had ever seen." Kwanona looked over at Mwasekera and smiled. "I told him that my wife and my sister made it."

Gafiyodi giggled a little behind her hand which she had raised to her mouth. She looked over at Mwasekera, who smiled into the fire that burned in the center clearing.

Kandiado spoke again. "We told him where we had dug our garden for the dry season, and he then gave us a fine hillside area for our gardens for the rainy season."

"It is at Mphemba Hill," Kwanona said eagerly. "We came near there when we returned, and so we stopped to see the place. It is fine. We will build more huts there. We will live here in the dry season, and there we can live when the great rains come. We will go there tomorrow to make ready for our garden. The rains are soon to come."

Kandiado looked into the fire. "And to think we worked so long for that hyena, Chikunda," he mused, "when freedom tastes so sweet and is so good! We are in luck. We will always have meat for food. The chief told us we could hunt all we wish. All we fear now are the slavers. But we will keep a watch all the time for them. I don't want another *gori* stick fastened to *my* neck. Indeed, I will die before I bow my back to slavery again."

Life settled down for the two families. The rains came and they all moved to their newly built mud houses near Mphemba Hill. Then they were kept busy for some weeks getting the gardens in good order and making little shelters for the chickens to protect them from wild animals.

The two families felt rich, moving about as they wished. They found many berries to pick, and the women dried them on leaves spread on the top of the huts. Gafiyodi gave birth to a baby boy soon after the move to Mphemba. The baby's arrival gave Kandiado much joy. Their other two little ones having sickened and died of whooping cough in Chikunda's village, and another babe later had been stillborn. But this little fellow was lusty and fat, and he soon became the pet of everyone.

Malinki, Mwasekera's son, could help with many tasks, and the little girl, Linnesi, was big enough to sit on a mat while her mother worked.

4

It seemed now as though they were secure. Surely the slavers would hardly think it worth their while to penetrate so deep into the bush for so few. But when Kandiado went to Apito's village again for the purpose of trading salt for more things, he heard the paralyzing news that Mpenzeni, the Angoni chief, was again at war; that great Arab dhows were on Lake Nyasa filling up with slaves caught by the dreaded Angoni warriors. Everyone seemed in a turmoil at Apito's village. No one felt safe. Kandiado traded all of the salt for weapons—spears and knives. He traveled only by night on his way home. It took him even longer than usual.

On the way home he killed a leopard and skinned it. The skin he gave to Gafiyodi and Mwasekera, who marveled at its beauty.

"Ah, this must be a good omen," Gafiyodi exclaimed, as she and Mwasekera cured the skin with salt and kneaded it to softness.

But Kandiado shook his head. "No, it cannot be a

good omen. I have news to bring you that is not good."
And he told them what he had heard in Apito's village.
He showed them the spears and the knives he had
brought back. "Who will be safe?" he asked sadly.

Mwasekera glanced around the little group. Then
she spoke up. "But let Kwanona tell you what he found
the other day while I was pounding the mealies. Tell
them, my husband."

Kwanona spoke in a low tone. "A cave! I found a
cave while you were away. A cave on the side of
Mphemba Hill. It is high, high up, and the mouth is so
covered by bushes that no one would know it was
there. It will be a good hiding place if we are in
danger."

Kandiado leaned forward. "A good hiding place?"

Kwanona nodded.

"Then we must get busy and store food there in case
we need it," Kandiado said.

They began at once to make preparations for an
emergency. "Even if no danger comes," Kwanona
said, "the cave will be a good cool place for the stor-
age of grain. Let's go up and clear the cave of wild
beasts or snakes."

The men took spears and torches and headed for
the cave. They carefully cleared a small amount of
the brush away from the opening, leaving enough to
hide the cave from the eyes of the enemy. A spring of
water welled up inside the cave itself. There would
be sufficient water for drinking and cooking.

Soon more disturbing news came to the two families,
news that slavers were prowling the area. They
moved into the cave immediately and began housekeeping in the roomy cavern. They lugged all of their

needed things up to the mouth of the cave. The little ones were carried up, while Malinki, sturdy and independent, stomped ahead, carrying a basket of mangoes on his head.

They fortified their place of refuge as well as primitive willing hands could do. Big stones were rolled close to the cave's mouth. Baskets of small ones lay in great heaps inside. They had drunk the dregs of the gall of slavery and were determined to resist it again —even to the death. But gardens had to be looked after, and the hungry needed to be fed, even though the fearsome menace hung over everyone. Water had to be fetched from the stream for washing clothes. The little spring flowing in the cave was used only for drinking water.

Mwasekera had not forgotten that she had once been caught in the garden hoeing, and when she thought of little Donda and her other little girl, gone for several years now, she seized Malinki to her breast so frantically that the little fellow cried out in fear, "What is the matter, Mother? What is the matter?"

"It is nothing," she would reply. "Only I love you so much that sometimes I am afraid. I am afraid some evil thing will happen to you."

With the eternal faith of childhood, the lad assured her gravely that he would be all right. "I am a big boy now, Amai," he would tell her. "See, I am very strong." With that he would thrash his small thin brown arms like windmills to convince her that he could put up a great fight if it were necessary to do so. She looked at him with great pride and then sighed heavily. If her little Donda were here, he would be just such a boy as this Malinki, sweet, gentle, and willing.

No woman or child ever ventured into the gardens unless one of the two men were stationed in one of the high trees on the lookout hill. It was a precaution they did not dare to do without. They agreed on a signal in case of danger. If Kandiado or Kwanona made the high chirruping noise which the *hluluhlulu* bird makes, then all must run for the cave without a moment of delay. So Malinki was never allowed to wander far, and Linnesi was kept tied to her mother's back while the hurried work of cultivating or reaping was going on.

Those days were fraught with worry, filled with burdens and fear. Even Malinki sensed it. In after years, whenever he heard the dovelike chirping of the *hluluhlulu* bird, he thought of the year they had spent in the darkness and damp of the cave on Mphemba Hill. He always felt an overwhelming sense of gratitude for the freedom from anxiety that came in his later years—freedom due much, he knew, to the work of the great David Livingstone.

Gradually the families gained confidence again and resumed normal life. Malinki grew bigger. Mwasekera fashioned a small loin cover from the bark and fibers of trees. The boy was too big to run about naked. Her busy fingers were always doing things for her children with the poor materials on which she could lay her hand. Tooth brushes from twigs; string from thick succulent leaves; blankets from bark. Nonetheless, the fear of being taken into slavery again never left them. Mwasekera dreamed again and again of her little boy, Donda, and of the evil face of Chikunda. Then she would awaken trembling, her face bathed with tears.

5

How could these poor ones have known that day was breaking in Africa? For David Livingstone had started an avalanche of change. He had gone back to England and told the people there in no uncertain tones that the teaching of the Bible alone was not enough. An example had to be set. The peoples of Africa were caught in a hopeless web. Legitimate trade had to be started in that vast center of the Dark Continent. Unless goods were brought into central Africa by legitimate traders and traded or sold for products of the country, slavery would continue to flourish. "Legitimate trade is a great necessity," Dr. Livingstone stressed. He pled for honest men to bring honest trade to the country. "Do not come as cruel fortune hunters," he begged.

Now the only way that the Angoni peoples, the Ajawas, and the other powerful tribes could obtain those things which they coveted—guns, bullets, iron pots, steel knives, and the like—was by bartering in human lives. To have a constant supply of slaves for

barter meant constant wars, with the attendant mis-
eries and agonies. But slowly, slowly this would
change. By the power of his magnetic personality,
Dr. Livingstone succeeded in waking up a number of
people in Great Britain, and he returned to Africa with
a heart full of hope.

The African Lakes Company was founded in direct
response to an appeal made in Britain by the missionary-explorer himself. From his journeys up and
down the Shire and Zambezi Rivers, Livingstone found
that the two conditions essential for the abolition of
the terrible slave trade in Africa were the gospel of
Jesus Christ and legitimate trade.

Two young Scotsmen, John and Frederick Moir,
who heard David Livingstone's appeal, decided to
lend their young strength to the opening of the Dark
Continent to civilization. It may be noted here, with
truth, that the British Empire owes some of its finest
and most lucrative acquisitions—nay, even its existence—not to kingly ambition nor diplomatic inter-
ventions, but to the efforts and sacrifices of common
men; indeed, to many men whose very memories
have perished; men who went forth, lured by adven-
ture, trade, or religion, and opened up vast tracts of
land hitherto inaccessible.

The two Moir brothers set out to penetrate the very
heart of Africa. Their primary aim was to open up a
trade between the district around the great lakes of
Nyasa and Tanganyika and the coast. They hoped to
find natural waterways on which to transport trade
goods.

If they could establish trade, carrying with them
things greatly needed in this primitive land, and if

they could make transportation convenient and easy, then slave gangs used to bear ivory and ebony would become unprofitable.

Several influential men in Glasgow, Scotland, and in London, England, joined together to support this trade venture of the young Moir brothers. Negotiations were entered into with manufacturers and produce brokers which continued through the years.

It was not as if the Moir brothers knew nothing of Africa. They had been in East Africa previously and had worked with a group of men building a road from Dar es Salaam to Lake Tanganyika. Both men were acquainted with the type of life one lives in the tropics.

The new trading company became known as the Livingstonia Central Africa Company, Limited. The Moir brothers were appointed managers. They set out on the long, long journey by ship, with suitable equipment which they knew they would need. A lake vessel, later named *Nyasa Lady*, was stored in sections in the hold. The Church of Scotland Mission promised to share its boat, the *Ilala*, with the new company. These lake steamers would carry immense quantities of goods to barter for ivory, rubber, and other products of the country which would be useful to the mother country across the sea.

After an adventurous journey up the Zambezi from the coast they finally came to the place where the Shire joined its swift waters with the Zambezi. The men cruised up the Shire and finally picked a high point some three miles from Chigumula, a busy Yoa village. Here they decided to build their trading post, The African Lakes Corporation. Bricks were made and a strong foundation built. Portions of the foundation and walls remain to this day. The vast enclosure, 126 feet long by 30 feet wide, served not only as a trading post but as a fort as well. A fort was needed in those times of war, slavery, and senseless slaughter. The old corner lookout towers were removed only within the last few years and the slots through which guns were fired have been filled in with bricks, but the vast enclosure and the buildings remain much as they were. Many a traveler or adventurer in those days gratefully spent a night or two within the safety of the post. Here one found not only safety but hospitality.

The African people of that area have a custom of giving names to strangers relating to impressions they have made, and since John Moir wore spectacles in which the people saw themselves reflected as in a mirror, they referred to him as *Mandala*, a Cinyanja word meaning reflection. The post became dubbed Mandala after the man who wore the glasses and who was the stronger character of the two brothers. This first post then became known as "Top Mandala," the name staying with it until this day.

Frederick, John's brother, always wore a beard, and he became known as Mr. Big Beard. His name in the Cinyanja language was *Ce Ndebvu*.

Today Mandala stores are scattered the length and breadth of that long narrow country. It may be said to their splendid credit that they were the only trading company in Nyasaland which did not deal in spiritous liquors.

A house, the dwelling place of the Moir brothers and their families, was erected at one end of the enclosure. Built in 1882, this large structure, two stories high with dining and drawing rooms and a number of spacious guest chambers, became a stopping place for all the missionaries, explorers, and traders who came into the area during those early days.

The Africans stood in wonder when they saw Mandala House or heard about it from those who worked there. There were mats with legs upon which the Europeans, whom the Africans called *Azungu*, slept. They were homemade beds, the springs being of laced cowhide to which the hair still adhered. These laced springs were topped by ponderous, lumpy homemade mattresses.

All the water used at the big house had to be carried from the stream some distance away. Before using it, the servants placed it in huge pots and boiled it and then strained it. This too the Africans thought very strange.

But the house itself was the biggest marvel, so accustomed were they to their own low wattle-and-daub huts. Many of them would walk for miles to come to the place where the *Azungu* had built "one house upon another" as they referred to the two-storied home. An outer staircase led to the upper porch. The Africans pointed and talked in hushed tones as they gazed at this staircase. They would cross deep, swift-flowing rivers; they would risk meeting a rhino or a crocodile, but to walk up the *Azungu's* steps—Ah! That was something else. A few, with great fear and trembling, crawled on hands and knees up the wide steps. Most of them shook their heads. "What could this be, a trap or a trick?" "With all the space available why did these people from a strange land put one house on top of another?"

The *Azungu* and their way of building were talked

about throughout the country, the news being carried by word of mouth and beat of drum.

The high walls surrounding the post proved to be a protection for the people in the subsequent terrible wars of the Angoni tribe. And here in the courtyard the porters who carried Mandala goods from the river steamer at Chiromo to the Top Mandala store gathered.

These carriers, a sturdy lot, brave and fearless and proud of their important position, faced the untamed bush, teeming in those days with wild animals, slavers, and other hostile natives, while they carried their cargo to and from Chiromo.

Mandala as an institution was particularly significant in Nyasaland history. Through this post legitimate trade was established on a solid and permanent basis and the slave trade finally crushed.

At fairly regular intervals runners arrived at Top Mandala with the news: *"M'steamer lifika! M'steamer lifika!"*

Then the fort became a bustling center of activity for the arrival of the steamer meant mail from the homeland and new goods to stock the shelves of the store. Traders, hunters, prospectors, missionaries, and the native people all looked forward to the news, *"M'steamer lifika!"*

Carriers quickly arranged their sixty-pound bundles on their heads and started off at a trot. Village people followed the carriers, also bringing ebony, ivory, rubber, rice, and the like to be traded for the strange things which came from lands across the seas. Soap, a wondrous commodity for those who had always used the sudsy juice of sisal and papaya leaves with which to wash their meager clothing and even their bodies; matches, a miracle indeed; watches, wondrous things; sugar and treacle, a tasty treat; cloth, something of worth and beauty; mirrors, a marvel—such innovations seemed so strange that the whole village would talk about them by the hour. They summed it all up as being magic—unexplainable magic. They were left breathless with the wonder of it all.

Not being used to the regular routine of work, the African was slow to see the necessity of doing anything regularly and on time. Meeting a deadline seemed so unnecessary. Then, too, there had been so many who had broken their promises to the black people that it was hard to put one's trust in the traders, missionaries, and others. Had they not often pretended one thing and then done another? True, David Livingstone was a good, kind, sincere man. In him the African put his trust. But a certain relative, they sadly learned, was not to be trusted. Then there was one called Fenwick who came to the Blantyre Mission as carpenter but who later worked for Mandala. He was determined to amass a fortune for himself and so concluded that he would become a trader in both rum and ivory. The Mandala store would not deal in liquor, and Fenwick was asked to leave.

Later Fenwick, in a furious outburst of temper, shot Chipatula, a chief of the Makololo people. The outraged tribesmen killed Fenwick in turn. Serious trouble ensued. Because of this man's act, trade was greatly hampered. For a time the river was closed to both trade and travel. Mandala suffered a great shortage of goods.

The African Lakes Company was blamed for the affair. However, Mandala people reminded the tribesmen that Fenwick had, at the time of the shooting, no connection with the company. He had been let go. They did not deal in liquor. They did not sanction Fenwick's action. But it was hard for the African to believe. Whom could he trust? Such men as Fenwick, and a relative of the famous missionary and explorer, did great harm to the cause of right in Africa.

The intrepid Moir brothers endured all kinds of hardships to establish trade in Nyasaland. And at last the sun began to set on the slave trade. It was too bad that David Livingstone could not have lived to see the glad day for which he had dreamed and labored so long. He had given his life for this, but by then the great slab had been pried up near the front of Westminster Abbey to admit his crudely wrapped, shrunken, dried-up body, which had been carried by loving bearers across Africa and sent home to England for burial. But that for which he had practically burned out his life was at last being accomplished.

Probably some who feel it their duty to debunk and minimize all good, will seek to destroy the work of David Livingstone. But no one could ever make Malinki believe that. He had tasted slavery and had seen the vast difference Livingstone's unselfish life made on his country. To those who had tasted such bitterness, freedom is lovely beyond belief. Gratitude, a rare and lovely quality, made Malinki into the unusual and outstanding man he was.

6

Most African men married long before reaching thirty years of age, but Malinki, probably already in his mid-thirties had not married. At that time, to people of central Africa, the year's end or beginning meant little. They knew time by the year of the drought or famine, period of the flooding or the occurence of an earthquake. One might say of an event, such as the birth of a child, that it was born at corn tasseling time, or at the time of grass burning. Times were still perilous and uncertain. The slave trade between tribes and Ajawa traders thrived in Africa even long after the Civil War in America had ended.

But now Mwasekera and Kwanona spoke to Malinki about taking a wife.

Look around, my son," Mwasekera urged. "We will pay a good dowry for the girl of your choice."

But Malinki shook his head. He remembered a friend, Kasonga by name, whom he had met, and the story Kasonga had told about being taken as a slave at the village Tsapa. He had had the *gori* stick fastened about his neck. He had heard the screams of his friends, and he had seen the flames from his village. His wife and babe had been taken from him.

He never saw her nor their babe again, for they were driven in different directions. He turned to see her being shoved into line. She could not look back. Then the forest closed in around her.

Kasonga had not been taken to Zanzibar, but driven to Bwani, a place hundreds of miles eastward on the banks of the Indian Ocean. Here a wealthy Swahili slave holder bought him, and he was put to work on a huge sisal plantation. He remained at this place in slavery for several years, until he and some of his fellow sufferers ran away and faced toward Nyasaland and home. After many weeks of hunger, thirst, and weary traveling the party came within sight of Mount Mlanje on the border of Nyasaland. Kasonga fell to the ground and wept and kissed the hard-packed earth repeatedly. He was near Tsapa—lovely Tsapa on the Namichamba River. Maybe, he thought, his father and mother might still be alive! But at Tsapa he found nothing but ruins. He found trees growing out of ruined huts. The bush was swiftly taking over, but it was home for the weary returned slave man just the same. All this he had told to Malinki.

Malinki shook his head, remembering Kasonga's story. How could he marry and have the dread of having his loved one snatched from him?

One day a messenger came breathlessly to the small village near Mphemba Hill where Malinki lived with Mwasekera, Kwanona, and the others. The messenger said that the chief of Kasisiland, the good chief who had given them their home and gardens and seeds, had started to barter his people for guns and cloth.

Where now could they turn? Where could they go? Kwanona wondered.

The messenger went on to tell about Dr. Scott from the Church of Scotland Mission near Blantyre, who came to Kasisiland and talked with the chief. He had described to the chief the wickedness and the cruel horrors of slavery. He was able to point out that legitimate commerce *had* already been started in Blantyre, that guns and bullets, cloth, soap, and sugar could be had in exchange for wood, fowl, mealies, skins, antelope meat, rhino horns, elephant tusks, and even labor, rather than human beings. The messenger then added, "Dr. Scott has sent out word to all the villages that those who wish to learn should come to the new mission station situated about a mile from the Mandala Fort."

The people talked this over amongst themselves. Should they trust these people from across the waters? Might this be a trick to spirit them away? Who could say what might become of their children should they send them to this mission?

But Mwasekera, who had endured much and suffered more than most people in her lifetime, turned her big brown eyes on Malinki, her grown son, and said, "You, my son—you must go. If there is some good thing to be had from these white ones, I want you to have it. You have ever been a good and loving son to me and to your father."

Malinki looked down at her hand placed on his arm. Many tiny laced scars showed that she had been no stranger to the cruel *chikoti*. A strong resolve formed in his mind. He *would* go, he would learn, and perhaps with some of his strength he could get some things such as his mother had never had. A cloth, perhaps, and a bright *mpanga* to tie around her head. "I will go, *Amai*. Maybe I can become important and perhaps I can do some great thing in this world." Malinki, although not a tall man, stood up to his full height, and his eyes lighted up with eagerness and determination. He looked into his mother's face. He could see the proud happy expression on her face, and then sadness seemed to come over her.

"What is it, *Amai?*" Malinki asked.

"Ah, I am thinking of my other little son stolen so long ago by the wicked slavers. Where is he today? Dead? Or alive working someplace in bonds and slavery, enduring the *chikoti*, and hunger and thirst?"

"Do not grieve, *Amai*. I will make it all up to you. You will forget all your past misfortunes. You just wait and see." Malinki, not daring to show his true feelings, walked away.

It did not take much effort for Malinki to get ready for school. His few possessions rolled up in a bamboo mat, he carried on a stick over his shoulders. A barkcloth blanket, a piece of the same material to wrap about his loins, a couple necklaces made of the claws of leopards and a charm to tie around his waist to prevent dysentery, with these Malinki left for school. With his ready mind and willing heart, how could anyone go better equipped?

7

What are now paved roads were in 1884 native paths beaten by countless generations of bare feet. Motor cars now whizz by where once the lion trod in undisputed majesty. Bridges span sluggish rivers where crocodiles once basked on muddy banks while waiting in evil patience for some prey. Trees where leopards were wont to climb have been felled to accommodate the growing, stretching towns of Blantyre and Limbe. If only some of the hardy old traders who had the barest of necessities, lugged eighty to a hundred miles on the heads of native carriers, could awaken! Even the crudest of stores would seem luxurious, for here now are bright prints, wide laces, hanks of fluffy wool, and flowery teapots and cups and saucers made in India and England. And here now are filling stations, bus stops, a beauty parlor, a bakery, a mill, hotels, and stores full of nylon, polyesters, silks, and other luxuries.

Would David Livingstone approve of all that has happened to his beloved Africa if he should awake today from his dusty tomb? No doubt he would shake his head sadly, for the white man does not bring only good. Only a few sunken graves with tipsy stones remind one of men who lived and died to wrest Nyasaland, now Malawi, from a trackless wilderness. Only here and there a native still lives, wracked with age, rheumy eyes nearly blind with the glaring sunshine of a hundred seasons, who remembers when Nyasaland was wilderness, still plagued by the lurking slaver. But malaria, dysentery, bilharzia, and a dozen other ailments have mowed down nearly all of those. The ones who now tread the paved streets have forgotten. They wear shoes, trousers, shirts, and even underwear, of which their forefathers knew not a thing. Countless generations before them trod the harsh rocky paths with bare feet and their loins gird about by a piece of bark cloth.

Malinki came on foot to the Church of Scotland school, which was made of wattle and daub, and had a grass roof. In the dormitory his bed was but a mat on the floor. At night the lions and the leopards ranged the environs of the mission and roared and coughed. The students heard and trembled as they had done hundreds of times in their own village. The bushland beyond the school teemed with danger and death in those days.

Those white men of the mission had started to build a church where they could worship their God. Malinki stared in amazement when he saw the size of the church measured out on the ground. He had been so used to littleness and to squalor. What would such a place as this be like?

Soon Malinki was set to work on the building. He,

with others, went to a place where good brick clay could be found. They began to carry pots of water on their heads from the stream to the place of good brick clay. The water was emptied onto the clay while the students mixed and mixed endlessly with their bare feet. They pulled out flaws such as small stones or clods that their bare feet discovered. They worked and worked, mixing and mixing. Tramp, tramp, sl-l-l-k, sl-l-l-k, calloused feet slushed up and down in the oozy red mud to make it smooth. Then the white men brought small wooden boxes. Into these boxes the students learned to pack the mud—not too wet, not too dry. Later they emptied them out where the sun would thoroughly dry the clay. Then these dried bricks were placed in the kiln and fired, making them tough as clay pots. The workers made up a little song which they sang as they worked, keeping time with their movements in perfect unison.

Tipanga-panga njerwa-njerwa! Njerwa!
Tipanga-panga njerwa-njerwa-lerodi!

For years they worked on the beautiful church, which still stands as a symbol of the struggles of those early days at the Blantyre Mission. The boys had never been accustomed to continuous or compulsive toil in their own villages. The way of the white missionary, his urgency to keep them working on a schedule, surprised and angered them not a little at times.

Young men would work a day—even part of a day —then take themselves off to bask in the rough grass by their villages, or go off hunting with bows and arrows, knobkerries, and tick-bitten dogs, as was their custom. But Malinki stayed by, and a few indomitable ones like him. Those who stayed on learned English, and they learned to read and write in both the Cinyanja and English.

One day Henry Henderson, one of the headmen at the mission, stopped by Malinki and asked, "What do you intend to do with your education? You and Golden here are the only two who began and who have stayed on. Now, what are you going to do?"

"Ah, bwana, I want to teach," Malinki answered, his eyes shining. He could think of nothing greater to do than his schoolmasters were doing for him.

"But Malinki," Henry Henderson protested, "there is no money; there are no schools! How can you teach when there is no place for you?"

"Bwana, my people are dying from the ignorance which is burning them. Look at me! I must be about forty years of age! I have never married for fear of the slavery business! There are many like me who want to learn. Who will teach them? You people cannot be everywhere."

"Yes, that is true," Henderson answered thoughtfully. "You have spoken truly, Malinki. You study hard and learn, and one day we'll give you a certificate. Then when the way opens, you will be ready. Perhaps the Lord is calling you to a greater work than you know. There's a text in the Bible about those who are not quitters," he confided.

"What is it?" Malinki asked, always amazed that the Bible contained so much.

" 'He that shall endure unto the end, the same shall be saved.' " Henry Henderson quoted.

8

Into the Africa a few years before the turning of the century—an Africa full of the acrid scent of wood and cow dung fires, of humming mosquitoes, and even of sudden death—came one called Joseph Booth, a religious man of the Seventh Day Baptist persuasion. Booth had been born in England but had gone to Australia at an early age. He came to Africa as the result of a taunt from an atheist in Melbourne. Booth had accepted a challenge to a debate regarding Christianity with a Mr. Symes. He felt sure he was able to meet the arguments of an atheist. Booth had heard Robert Ingersoll several times in his life, and he felt that if he did not stand up for Truth, he would be remiss in his duty to the Lord.

The atheist, seeing his arguments were met and refuted with a degree of convincing, intelligent reasoning, resorted to personality derision and the unanswerable fire of sarcasm.

"Mr. Booth," he jeered, "by your avowed love for Jesus Christ, I judge you are going to follow His commands. Christ said to the rich young man, 'Sell all that thou hast.' And to all His followers, 'Go ye into all the world, and preach the gospel.' Of course you will follow the words of your Master. You're a rich young man. When is the sale to be, Mr. Booth? I want to be there."

As a result of this barrage of ridicule, Mr. Booth did just that—sold his possessions—and prepared to leave for Africa. His wife died only three weeks before the date of his sailing to his selected field of labor. He took his little daughter, Emily, and sailed for Africa. His son Eddie was attending college in England.

The first home of the Booths was a mud hut with the usual mud floor and leaky grass roof. Their furniture consisted of packing boxes. It had not been fully established that the mosquito was the culprit that caused malaria fever, so they were fully exposed to the cause of sudden death in this country that was all too often the "white man's grave." In these primitive circumstances, with a small ten-year-old girl to look after, with malaria a frequent visitor, they sorely needed a houseboy. They needed him for the chores of fetching food and water, for building fires and washing clothes —and to care for them when they became ill.

The first ventures in hiring houseboys were disastrous. The boys proved to be entirely unreliable, ignorant, and dirty. Spoons, knives, forks, and provisions disappeared with astounding regularity. And then John Chilembwe, an intelligent young Yao, presented himself. In broken English he requested employment. He seemed honest and willing to learn as well as being eager to help. The Booths took him into their home. It was a wondrous relief to find in John exactly what they needed. He proved to be trustworthy, honest, energetic, and he had obtained a small smattering of education at some place. He could read a little, write some, and speak haltingly in English. There is some evidence that he went to the Church of Scotland Mission school in Blantyre, but nothing is conclusive.

John knew much that the Booths did not know. He knew the danger to missionaries if they did not boil their drinking water. He knew how and where to get food, how to plant gardens in that area, how to make a fire without matches, and what to do when one came down with malaria and dysentery.

The Booths, Joseph and little daughter Emily, depended on John for everything. He was pridefully tireless in his service for them. He cooked, foraged for food, made gardens, and carried and boiled water. He held their pallid hands and heads when paroxysms of vomiting from gastric malaria came upon them. He carried their sweat-soaked clothing to the stream to beat it clean with the aid of crude bars of soap. The Booths would have perished without him. They could not have managed without faithful John.

Even in the comparative isolation of the Shire Highlands, the feeling of uncertainty and change was in the air. Even into the Shire Highlands were coming strange men who were not living the religion of the good David Livingstone. They were not living the life of those who were in charge of the missions or even of the gentle Joseph Booth.

Booth had deep convictions against killing, even in times of war, so this is what made it strange that later some blamed him for starting a murderous insurrection in central Africa that caused trouble for many

years to come. He became a man whom the missionaries resented, for he did not agree with the prices
they paid for commodities, or with wages, or yet with
the way that the native people were treated. He seemed
to have an earnest desire to make them less cringing
and subservient and to prepare them for carrying responsibility.

Vast tracts of land were being taken by men, and
not for mission purposes, but for gain. A. L. Bruce, a
brewer, strangely enough, had married Agnes Livingstone, the daughter of the great missionary. Another
Livingstone, a distant relative, took vast tracts of land
near Mitsidi. Mr. Livingstone's later unjust treatment
of John Chilembwe was unworthy of a relative of the
great man and probably did more to foment rebellion
than anyone else's actions.

It was not only in Africa that storms were in the air.
Science and knowledge were increasing everywhere
and with that, instead of ease that additional riches
could give, came corrosive greed. European countries sprawled uneasily, demanding more space,
cheap labor, and raw material. Ships plowed the seas
searching for material for the factories the industrial
revolution had precipitated into a world ill-prepared
for such gigantic moves.

Steam multiplied the production of goods and the
speed of movement. Old sail ships were fast becoming
obsolete. But in Africa the old ways held sway. Oxen
creaked by with huge-wheeled, clumsy wagons.
Men still tilled the soil as their ancestors had for four
thousand years. But the time of change was near,
very near.

Land-hungry, riches-hungry fortune hunters came,

ruthlessly robbing and oppressing and exploiting the people. The gentle Mang'anja and the bold Yao and Angoni were confused. They had seen the best and the worst in white men.

Soon after Joseph Booth's arrival, word came to the Church of Scotland Mission that a missionary had come to Mandala House who was inquiring for African teachers. He had a small daughter with him and had come from across the seas.

"Now is your chance," Henry Henderson said to Malinki. "Go and see this man. They say he has money which he wishes to invest in building up mission work. He may build the school you want so badly. You may realize your ambition quicker than you think. We will give teacher's certificates to you and Golden. Take them to this man whose name is Booth. This may be your chance to have a school. And may God bless you, Malinki."

9

Eagerly Malinki and his friend Golden, who had started at the mission school the same time as Malinki, set out to see Joseph Booth. They carried their teacher's certificates carefully. Each man wore a piece of calico wrapped around his hips and each had a necklace made of leopard teeth. They had combed their bushy hair with crude wooden combs, and they felt quite presentable. They set out walking a day's journey to Mandala House.

Upon arriving at their destination, the two stood a distance from the door, squatted down, and called out, "*Odi! Odi!*" according to African courtesy. Soon a servant boy came out to ask them what they wanted.

"We want to see Bwana Booth," Malinki stated.

"But it will be useless to see him," the boy protested. "He can't speak Cinyanja!"

"Then I will talk to him in English," Malinki stated firmly.

"Are you able? Are you able?" the boy asked in astonishment.

5—M.O.M.

"Yes, go and get him." Malinki waved his hand a little proudly.

The boy seemed quite impressed that Malinki could speak English.

In a few minutes, Joseph Booth came out on the wide porch. Malinki saw that he was a short man of perhaps fifty. He wore a dark suit and a cloth around his neck.

With trembling hands, Malinki and his friend showed this stranger their precious teaching certificates. Mr. Booth read them quickly and then looked from one to the other applicant. "Whose certificates are these?" he asked, quickly, tapping the certificates with his finger. "You must have stolen them. Surely you cannot qualify."

"They are ours, bwana," Malinki spoke up in the English language. "You can ask our bwana! He can tell you we went to the mission school."

Mr. Booth took an envelope and a pencil from his pocket. "Write your name," he commanded.

Malinki took the pencil and paper and wrote firmly "Morrison Malinki," for it had occurred to him that most people had two names. He handed the paper and pencil to his friend who wrote "Golden Mathaka."

Mr. Booth stood looking at the neat signatures with pleased surprise showing on his face.

Malinki ventured a question then, "Bwana, why did you doubt us?"

Mr. Booth looked a little sheepish. "Your clothes— ah—are so shabby. Not at all like an educated person should—ah—wear. But come, let us give you a little examination." With that, the two were given sums and were asked many questions. Evidently the answers pleased Mr. Booth, for suddenly he leaped to his feet. "John! John!" he called.

An African man dressed like Joseph Booth appeared. Malinki and Golden were introduced to him, John Chilembwe, the very man who was later to write a dark page in the history of Nyasaland, the one who was to spoil Joseph Booth's good name and turn the educational efforts of godly missionaries into high disfavor for a long time.

"Come, John," Mr. Booth said, "help me outfit these men so they'll look like real teachers."

They went into Joseph Booth's room in Mandala House. There a great trunk stood by the bed. Mr. Booth opened it. Malinki held his breath. John Chilembwe took out two white coats, two pairs of white trousers, and two shirts for each young man. Then lifting up the tray, he brought out shoes which were fitted to their feet.

"Take these men to the stream, John, so they can bathe before they put on the clothing." Mr. Booth said.

After washing at the stream, Malinki and Golden looked at the clothing laid out for them. They touched the pieces gingerly. Malinki held up a shirt, upside down. He shook his head. Then he looked at Golden, who seemed as confused as he. Finally John Chilembwe helped them dress, for they could not make heads or tails of this strange wearing apparel.

When once more they stood before Joseph Booth, Malinki could not think of a word to say, although he knew they should give this man a big thank-you.

Mr. Booth scrutinized the men. Then he cleared his throat and began to speak. "As teachers," he said, "you must ever be an example in all things." He began to walk back and forth as he talked. "You must be a good example in dress, in cleanliness, in behavior, and in speech." He paused and stopped in front of Malinki. "I am going to Matsidi to buy land for a mission. You must meet me there in a month. Do you understand?"

"Yes, we understand," Malinki spoke up.

A month later Golden Mathaka and Morrison Malinki met Mr. Booth at Matsidi. There was much work to be done. Houses had to be built. That meant poles had to be cut. A pit was dug over which to place logs chopped to length from tree trunks. The logs were then roughly sawed into boards. Malinki and Golden spent many days, one in the pit and the other above, using the crude saw, pushing it up and down, up and down through the logs placed lengthwise across the pit. Mud had to be mixed for daubing walls and for the making of bricks. The buildings had to be completed before the teachers could start teaching.

10

Up to this time Malinki had had very few thoughts
of marriage. His life had been too full of perplexing
things to even hope for much happiness for himself.
But now things were changing. Gradually, slave raids
had grown less and less as the missionaries and the
white traders came in and settled. Paths grew into
roads leading to towns. The people began to breathe
a little easier and to plant with some hope of reaping.
Malinki began to teach in the little school he had built.
Then in the village where he taught, he saw a maiden
whom he fancied greatly. Her skin was light-brown
in color. She had merry, sparkling eyes, and a lithe,
lovely body. Of course she was unlettered. There was
no other kind! But Malinki determined to teach her to
write! He told Mr. Booth of his plan to marry this girl,
and Mr. Booth agreed to help him. He took Malinki
into the Mandala Store to buy some cloth for a wedding gift after the dowry would be arranged.

"Now you go to her village and make the arrangements for your marriage," Mr. Booth counseled.

It never occurred to Malinki to ask the girl whether or not she would like him. It just wasn't done. The old marriage planners were consulted, and they agreed very readily, for Malinki was an impressive figure with his white trousers and coat and shirt and shoes. The day of the marriage was planned, and Malinki gave the girl the length of red cloth he had purchased.

His bride trembled when Malinki gave her the cloth. No other girl ever had such a cloth for her wedding. And no girl ever had such a fine husband with such shoes, such clothes, and such knowledge stuck up into his head, the bride assured him.

It is a custom in some tribes to give a wife a new name at the marriage, so Malinki, at his marriage, gave the pretty maiden the name Deriza Rachel. Then he took her to Matsidi where he built a home of mud and poles for her.

Soon after Malinki and Deriza Rachel's marriage exciting news came—news that missionaries were coming from England! "There are five families and two single men. Think of it! Five families!" Mr. Booth exclaimed to Malinki.

Some weeks later a great shout arose. The carriers struggling with the bulky machilas and other heavy loads came to Matsidi. The travelers, weary, thirsty, hungry, and dirty, and some ill, had arrived. Malinki watched the excited Mr. Booth, who seemed hardly able to speak.

Then Malinki turned his attention to the carriers, who wore only coarse loincloths tucked cleverly between their legs and tied securely in hard knots. Sweat glistened and trickled down their gleaming bodies, making tiny rivulets in the red dust. Their hair stood out in bunches, each bunch separate like little nodules of wool. The carriers stood there, patiently awaiting the "soap and cloth" with which they were paid for carrying these white ones in the machilas all the long miles from Chiromo. Malinki thought of other days when men like these had been whipped and forced on journeys not at all of their choosing and with no pay at the end of their journey.

The journey made by the missionaries from their beloved homeland had taken many weeks.

With the coming of every white missionary, with every effort made on the part of England and America, the slave traffic was driven farther and yet farther from this tiny country of Nyasaland in central Africa. The missionaries also brought in undreamed-of chances—chances for progress, for education, for enlightenment—never yet thought of by the tribes about Lake Nyasa.

Those who came to Matsidi were the Hamilton family, Dr. Allen and family, the William Miller family, the Hawkins family, the Dieth family, Mr. Lindsay, and Mr. Mackett. After they had rested a few days, they were located at the places where they were to labor. They would learn much in the next few months. Life would be very different from that they had left. They would learn to sleep on hard, lumpy beds whose springs were woven cowhide strips. They would learn to conserve water, for it was all carried a long distance in pots on the heads of servants. Then, too, water became very scarce in the dry season. One learned quickly to save every drop. Often it came the color of coffee, for it had to be scooped out of almost dry waterholes.

Malinki himself was used to the scarce supply of water. But he thought a great deal about the places where the missionaries slept. He had never slept upon a bed and a spring. Always he had slept on a mat. It could be rolled up or spread out anywhere. Surely this was more agreeable than the bulky beds the missionaries seemed to put so much store by.

Not long after the arrival of the missionaries at Matsidi, Malinki was sent to a place two miles away called the Zambezi Industrial Mission. Here he built a two-room, mud-and-pole hut and established the Malinki home which has stood now for many years. One of his pupils in the beginner's class was the brown-eyed, slim Deriza Rachel, his girl-wife whose bright young eyes hardly left her teacher-husband as he stood before the class. And he was gratified to find her at the head of every class seizing at every grain of learning just as the fowls seized quickly the mealies spilt in his dooryard.

A grown man with a sparse beard named Chikumbu joined the class, a man slow to learn but quick to quarrel. he was angered beyond measure when children excelled him in reading, writing, and doing sums.

One day, Malinki asked Chikumbu to read a list of words that had been written on the rough blackboard.

"The first word is 'akazi,' " Chikumbu said.

"Try again," Malinki suggested.

"It is 'akazi,' " Chikumbu replied stubbornly.

"No," answered Malinki. "Next."

"Mwana," answered a little fellow.

"You are right," the teacher answered.

Chikumbu arose in a towering rage. "And I say it is

'*akazi*'!" he shouted. "And who dares to refute me?"

"*I* dare," Malinki said quietly. "I am the master here, Chikumbu, and if you are not willing to learn, you may go home to your kraal and tend your goats. This is a school where we learn the right names for words and not to fight over the wrong names."

"What's this? What's this?"

The class all turned to see Missionary Miller standing in the doorway. Chikumbu stepped back and stood leaning against the wall.

The children began to explain what had happened.

William Miller went over to the man and tapped him on the chest. "We have no room for fighters or contradictors or troublemakers here. If I take you to the police, they will lock you up in jail for being a troublemaker. If you know more than the teacher, you better go start a school of your own. If you know less, then you must be still and try to learn."

In the end Chikumbu apologized and things went on smoothly again.

Deriza's dovelike eyes never left her husband's face. Malinki saw she kept clasping and unclasping her slender hands. "Do not quarrel, dear one. Do not make the quarrel!" her eyes seemed to be pleading.

Malinki knew why her tender heart was fearful. She had suffered much. But he knew that he had to be the master of his school. And though he was small of stature and slight of build, he was determined to keep good order. And so school went on.

One day Malinki said to Deriza Rachel, "When school is out and vacation comes, I shall work for the Mandala people. They told me I could be supervisor of the carriers, and I could go along and see to their food and see that none run away with the loads. There was much trouble when they did not have an honest supervisor."

Even though Malinki was small in stature, he had a commanding personality. The carriers were superstitious; and when they saw him reading directions even in the strange *Angelezi* (English) language, and then taking a stick and a piece of white stuff and making marks to send back which seemed to talk to the receiver, they were awed. They were afraid to steal any of the loads. The African Lakes Company wanted to hire Malinki permanently, but there was that certificate—a permission to teach—which put him far above even the best superintendent's class. He would not give up teaching.

As to his school pay, he had to take it in produce and in livestock. Money, as such, among most of the Africans of that day, was practically nonexistent. He would sit in his house when the parents came with their children. They were impressed when he wrote down their names and the names of the children on what he called paper. Then he would tell them what they were to bring for the fees for their children. Some had to bring things in each week or month. Things that were perishable had to be brought more often. Some who raised rice or millet could bring it in bags, and it would be the fee for quite a time to come.

There were some who were very poor and who had nothing to bring. These he put to work digging in his garden spot, cultivating and seeding it. Others carried water during the season when there was no rain. But he had to have something from everyone if he was to teach their children. He had not been taught psychology, but he knew in his humble way that a thing would be more valuable in the eyes of the people if it cost them something. Then he had a dim idea of the dignity of paying one's way. That was the way a new Africa must be built.

11

Back in Kasisiland, many days' journey from the Zambezi Industrial Mission, lived Mwasekera and Kwanona. They had lived there for many years. It was from there they had sent Malinki to learn to become a teacher. Mwasekera had lived with fear, pain, and injustice. She had known bereavements. She knew not a thing about prayer, or about the heavenly Father who is always aware of the anguish that sin has caused. Day by day she thought of her son, Malinki. "He will get much learning. He will be able to help our people. I will see him again," she told herself over and over. And when she thought of her son, Mwasekera was happy. Kwanona, her husband, was a good, kind, patient husband. She did not mind working hard to make living as easy for him as she could. But both Mwasekera and Kwanona sensed that there was something in the very air. There were vast changes being made in the world they had known so long.

Messages came to Mwasekera by word of mouth

from time to time, messages from Malinki. It gladdened her heart immeasurably. "I was told to tell you by your son, Malinki, that he is well and learning. Here is a gift for you."

And Mwasekera treasured not only the gifts but the words as well. It seemed that though Malinki was poor, he sent something with every message. Once it was a piece of blue soap he had managed to acquire. He sent her special instructions as to how it was to be used. "Do not eat it, *Amai.* Its color may be a fine blue, but it is for putting in water to take the dirt off the body. It can also be used instead of sisal for washing the clothes. You take your clothes to the stream and wet them with the water. Rub them with this piece of *sopo* till you see the bubbles come, and then beat the clothes on the stones. They will come cleaner, and the *sopo* will do the work quicker. If you use the *sopo* on your body, do not get any in your eyes if you can help it. Even though it does not blind you, it will hurt fiercely until you can get it washed out."

Another time he sent her an empty bottle that had been given to him by Mr. Booth. Malinki sent word that the bottle, being made of glass, would break in many pieces if it were hit or dropped. She must be very careful of it. Milk could be put into it, and it could be put into the stream to keep cool, and no cat could get into the milk in this bottle.

And the messenger brought back word to Malinki that Mwasekera had been pleased with the bottle. She had held it up and turned it this way and that. She had been very happy to receive the gift.

One day Malinki and Deriza Rachel sent Mwase-kera a length of calico to wear. It was a bright-orange with black dots on it. Mwasekera had had only two such pieces of cloth before. One had been given to her by her Angoni warrior husband, the father of Malinki, on her wedding day so long ago. The other piece of cloth had been sent to her by Apito, king of Kasisiland, in return for the gift of salt. Now, thanks to her wonderful son, she had a proper *nsaru* to wrap around her body when she went to market. She had never dreamed of having such a piece of calico again. She wrapped it in banana leaves and put it where the white ants could not destroy it.

Mwasekera sent back messages by word of mouth to her son. She told him of her great desire to see him and his wife. She sent her thanks for the many gifts.

"I am going to send for my mother and Kwanona to come here," Malinki told Deriza Rachel one day. "I will build a house near ours, and she and Kwanona can learn of the Christian faith. We ourselves have learned much. And they will learn that they never need be afraid anymore."

Deriza Rachel looked up at Malinki and smiled, "And when our little one is born, she can help me, for she knows a lot more about babies than I do." Deriza Rachel touched her swelling abdomen happily. "She will be proud of her grandchild, and so will Kwanona be glad. He looked on you as his real son."

"Aha, you are a good wife, Deriza Rachel," Malinki told her. "Mwasekera will love you. You will be good to her. She had never known much happiness, until we ran away from Chikunda."

"Oh, yes," Deriza Rachel whispered, "I will love her, for she will be my mother too—since my own mother is gone."

With the help of the strong students who mixed the mud, Malinki had a hut built with two rooms, just as he and Deriza Rachel had. To pay for his children's schooling the father of one of the students came and thatched the roof snugly and then built a kitchen house near at hand. Now Malinki waited for the first traveler going to the village where Mwasekera and Kwanona lived to send the message for them to come and be with him so he and his wife could care for them as the weakness of old age came upon them.

Malinki and Deriza Rachel waited for word from Mwasekera or for the arrival of the parents, now grown old.

Malinki was finishing the last class of the day when Kwanona and Mwasekera came. Kandiado was with them. He had helped carry all their stuff. He said that he wished to greet the good son who was wise and learned. Malinki finished his class and dismissed the school, and the children went to their homes with the wondrous tale that the teacher's parents had come.

Malinki and Deriza Rachel watched Mwasekera and Kwanona walk about clasping and unclasping their scarred hands. Tears streamed from Mwasekera's eyes as she saw it all—the two-roomed hut Malinki had prepared and a garden spot.

"This will be the church," Malinki told them, showing them where he had pegged out an oblong space in the grasses.

"And what is a church?" Kwanona asked.

Malinki knew he could not explain it all in a minute. He told them both that he had a wonderful Book he had received from the Church of Scotland Mission that told all about the great God who gave them their lives." He is the One who sends the rain and makes the trees and the crops to grow," Malinki told them. "He made the sun and the moon and the stars, the birds, the cattle—everything."

"Even the devils who are watching to bewitch and destroy us?" Kwanona asked cautiously.

"Even that I can explain, so you need not be afraid anymore." Malinki smiled. He looked forward to taking the ugly superstitions out of the lives of those he loved so dearly. "We have been believing many foolish things that are not true," he added. "I can bring to you the peace and joy that I have now."

"You mean you do not have to fear bad luck any longer? You are not afraid of some of the things we have been warned against like planting the mango or the coffee tree?" Kwanona asked in amazement. "You know we are always having to do things to appease the devils so they would not bring upon us suffering and death. You mean you do not believe in the 'smelling out'?"

Malinki's smile broadened as he looked first at his mother and then at Kwanona. "I know how you fear. Remember I was raised with you, and I remember childhood was marred with dreams of fear and terror. And, true, we had many things to fear from evil men, but not from devils as we thought. Of course there is a devil, who is an enemy of the great God, and of him I will tell you but I can also tell you how to make him keep away. Why, it took many days to quiet the fears of my wife, for superstitions are many. But now she is not afraid."

Mwasekera shook her head slowly. "She is with child now, and she must be careful about many things," she said wisely. "You know she must not touch any salt. That is very dangerous. I hope she has been very careful about that."

"There are not so many things to be afraid of as you think, Mother," Malinki spoke up. Many of the things you fear are heathen fears. The biggest thing we fear is dirt and filth which can harm a child very much. Then there are things a Christian does not eat. We did not know some of these things were very bad for us to eat—take rats and mice for example." Malinki paused a moment, and then he went on, "I am going to teach you about God, and you will lose many of your fears. There is a saying in the good Book: 'Perfect love casteth out fear.' "

Mwasekera looked worried. She laid her hand fearfully on Malinki's arm, "Do not run risks with this good wife while she is carrying your child, my son," she said in a voice full of fear. "There are many evils awaiting a child and a mother. Even though you say there is no danger, do not allow her to touch salt. I will be there to help her. I know that if a woman who is with child touches salt, she may bring death to her whole family. This is a teaching I have heard all my life."

Malinki smiled, but he did not laugh. He knew the fearsome superstitions that gripped his mother's mind. He remembered Kwanona talking to him when he was a child about the great bird that caused the thunder. When he had expressed unbelief, Kwanona was very positive. "My own grandfather saw it once. It was frightful," Malinki remembered hearing him say. He well knew it would take a long time to get rid of the superstitions that darkened the minds of Kwanona and his mother.

81

At last Mwasekera and Kwanona were settled in their hut. Malinki bought a blanket for them from Mandala. It was warm and soft and made from the wool of English sheep. He had bought some woven material and had a tailor make for Kwanona his first pair of trousers. Malinki smiled when he saw how proudly Kwanona wore the trousers instead of the rough bark cloth he had worn almost all his life. Malinki also had a shirt made for Kwanona.

A shirt with sleeves! Kwanona was speechless.

Malinki had to show him several times how to wear it. Malinki remembered his own bewilderment when a few short years before Booth had given him such clothes to put on. Now Kwanona put the shirt on upside down. They laughed together as Malinki showed Kwanona how to wear it. There was a great deal of joy and laughter in the two huts those days.

Kwanona soon learned to pack the red mud into the boxlike molds for the brick Malinki wanted to use to build the church. And Malinki and Deriza Rachel beamed as they saw Kwanona and Mwasekera learning little by little to live without fear as they learned about the Lord Jesus Christ. Both of them were also learning to live without hate.

One day Kwanona said, "Me, I would like to go back some night and choke the life out of Chikunda. I would like to tie his arms and legs with sharp threads and beat him with a *chikoti.*"

Malinki reached for the Bible which he called, "*Buku Lopatulika Ndilo Mau a Mulungu* [the Book which contains the Word of God]." He read words almost incomprehensible to Kwanona's mind. "Love your enemies, . . . do good to them that hate you, and pray for them which despitefully use you."

Kwanona stared, his mouth open with astonishment, and he shook his head. What kind of *Buku*—what kind of God would tell His people to love their enemies—to pray for people who do wicked tricks to you and torment you?

While the church went up slowly, Kwanona learned not only how to use the plumb bob to make walls straight, but he learned another plumb bob to make lives straight by following the Word of God. He also learned by the gentle conversation of Malinki that some of the superstitions that they had held so strongly were nothing but foolishness. Kwanona thought of the superstition about mango trees. Oh, how good that fruit is! How nice it would be to have a whole grove of mangoes near the house. The big flat seeds grew so easily! But one must never, never plant a mango. The witch doctor had assured them many times that if they did they would never live to eat the fruit of it. If they had not believed that silly superstition, they would have had a whole orchard bearing fruit now, in Kasisiland! But now—

But now, to his amazement, Kwanona saw that Malinki had planted a whole orchard of mangoes to the south of the huts not too far from the flourishing school. Mwasekera was terrified at first when Kwanona showed her the orchard; but when Malinki took her out and picked a few of the luscious fruits to show her the lie of it all, she felt better. Her wonderful son told her that such superstitions were of the devil. The devil wanted the people of Africa to remain in heathen darkness, Malinki said, and not come out into the marvelous light of truth. The devil was the maker of

83

chaos, but God was a God of love and order. He wanted His children to provide for themselves and family. Most of the superstitions they had learned about were not true. Malinki even now was picking great baskets of mangoes and other fruits from the orchards he had planted. Nothing evil happened.

And so the building and the happiness grew.

12

When Joseph Booth had come to Africa, he had established a mission some thirty-five miles from Blantyre where the Mandala House and the Church of Scotland Mission were located. The tract of land, 2001 acres, had been first sold by a Chief Makwiro to a German planter for a few bundles of cheap red cloth. The planter, who had built a couple brick houses on the land, sold it all to Mr. Booth who set out guavas, lemons, loquats, avocados, and banana trees near the houses for his own use. Coffee and sisal had also been planted, but Booth was not able to make the crops produce enough to make the mission self-supporting. Booth, although from Australia, had backers in America. They did not like the way Booth was working in Africa.

He had the highest intentions with a real desire to raise the standard of living and to improve the literacy rate of the people of central Africa. Some of his critics say he went too fast and put ideas that were not good into the African mind. Yet his intentions were good, and he aimed to do right. Perhaps it was because so many unprincipled men, like a swarm of locusts, came in to amass a fortune and to exploit the native peoples that the good done by Joseph Booth was misrepresented. But it must be said that Joseph Booth was sincere in what he did.

The Boers in South Africa under Oom Paul Kruger kept the black people "in their place," as the Dutch said. Oom Paul hated missionaries, for they spoke of black and white equality. South Africa was a long way from the interior, but, strangely enough, news traveled. There had been trouble for many years between the Boers and the English people. The Boers trekked away from their hated English invaders. They penetrated the interior of Africa like white fingers, thrusting menacingly into the very heart of Africa. Wherever the Boers went, with their high-wheeled wagons, their garden tools, and their agricultural equipment, they were resisted fiercely by the Africans with poisoned arrows and spears. But these native people, much as they tried, could not win. The white fingers clutched guns more powerful than the arrow and spear, and whole villages were wiped out. Unrest was all over the Dark Continent. It seemed that when good came in the person of the dedicated missionary, evil came in the wake of fortune hunters.

When Joseph Booth had come to Africa, he had had William Carey's idea of a self-supporting, self-propagating enterprise by which the African could learn and work and maintain a better standard of living than the generations of his ancestors had maintained. The dream may have been too big too soon. But he was looking about for an intelligent African man whom he could personally train to help him. He had the commendable ambition of helping Africans get training and education. He wanted to help them grow food and marketable crops, such as coffee, tea, rubber, sugarcane, and sisal. In this way, he reasoned, funds could be obtained to purchase those things which could not be grown or produced in Africa. He was far ahead of his time. Due to injustice and greed on every side, Joseph Booth was charged with the responsibility for the trouble that followed a few years later.

About this time a Mr. Alexander Dickie, who had been associated with Joseph Booth, John Chilembwe, and Morrison Malinki, asked a favor of Malinki. He wanted him to go along with him to pay a visit to the Angoni chief.

Of all the things Malinki had been asked to do this was the most dangerous. He realized that Mr. Dickie had no conception of the whims, unreasonable superstitions and caprices of any of the chiefs. Malinki tried to tell Mr. Dickie that with many of the chiefs human life was cheap, too cheap; and if any so much as bored or displeased his royal majesty, a horrible death was sure to follow. But the more Malinki tried to dissuade Mr. Dickie, the more determined he was to make the visit.

"It will be very dangerous," Malinki told him, realizing inwardly it was an understatement. "The chief is a very fierce and dangerous personage."

But at last Malinki agreed and began to make preparations. He had a heavy heart. When he told Deriza Rachel of the plan, she wept bitterly.

"Ah, I well know the danger. Perils from wild beasts

—lions, gliding serpents, stinging mosquitos, and evil men. How can I bear to have you, the one who has brought me more happiness than anyone in my life, thrust into such horrible danger?"

Malinki could hardly comfort her, for he, too, had dreadful premonitions. This chief who held the lives of his subjects in such careless hands was more despotic than any of the other African chiefs. Perhaps it was because he had hardened his heart to misery and anguish for so long in order to get the coveted English goods. To men to whom the spear, the bow and arrow, the bludgeon, and the knobkerrie had long been weapons, the long slim gun that breathed fire and death was a breathtaking miracle. He would do anything to get these guns. There were many who still felt they could make a double profit—slaves one way and trade stuffs the other. This was the agonizing situation that David Livingstone had found in central Africa. It still existed to a certain extent. Perhaps no man had ever done so much for so many as Livingstone did. To this day, even in remote villages, his name is respected.

It was against his will, but being afraid to express his fears and honest forebodings before the confident Mr. Dickie, Malinki prepared for a journey he knew could well be the last he would ever take. He would have liked to refuse, but the Church of Scotland Mission had done so much for him that it seemed to Malinki the height of ingratitude to refuse to go along with a man who had been connected with this mission.

Indeed, Mr. Dickie had done a great deal for Malinki personally. While building the school and the church at the mission, he had taken Malinki into his confidence more than any of the others. When he would bring out a tool that Malinki had never seen before, he would stop and explain it to him. "This is an auger," he would say, indicating the big tool with pride. "I don't suppose you ever saw one before."

"No, bwana," Malinki would reply, respectfully. "What does it do?"

"It makes holes in boards, when we need holes. This one makes big holes. Now this is another hole maker; it makes smaller holes. It is called a brace and bit."

"Bwana, why do you take this good wood and make holes in it?" Malinki would ask.

"Well, we need to put things together. When we make furniture and build houses, we have to have holes to put the big bolts through to hold things together so that they will not fall apart and perhaps injure people." The kind Mr. Dickie did not seem to mind explaining everything to the interested Malinki. Malinki's respect increased as he saw the quick work of the saw, the auger, and the brace and bit. He never tired of seeing the shavings curl up as Mr. Dickie's strong arms shoved the wood plane along on a board to make it satin smooth.

"See?" he would say as he would rub his thumbs on the surface of the board. "No splinters in that!"

"What is a splinter, bwana?"

"Ha, do you remember bringing me some boards to plane, and I had to take a small sharp piece of wood out of your hand?"

Malinki looked at the palm of his hand and shuddered. The place was still tender and sore. "Oh, yes, bwana!"

"Well, that was a splinter," Mr. Dickie told him. "We

do not want splinters to come off the tables and chairs and church pews to hurt people."

Then Malinki realized more fully what wonderful good this invention of the smoothing plane was for the people. He looked at the rolling curls of shavings with more respect and wondered at the wisdom of the *Azungu*.

Then there was the time when Mr. Dickie gave him a pair of black *kabadulos* or pants. He had been able to entirely discard the loin cloths he used to wear for work or gardening. It was wonderful to be clothed like this all the time. Yes, he must help the bwana, even though he was asking a fearful thing. Malinki strongly suspected that even Mr. Dickie did not realize the peril he was going into.

It took four carriers to convey Mr. Dickie's gear. He took blankets, a pillow, a large mosquito net, medicine, tea, coffee, a large tin of English biscuits, some meal for porridge, three cooking pots, some cups, spoons, knives, sugar, soap, oil, and ever so many things. There were two guns, some wadding, shotgun shells, and some gunpowder. There were bottles of medicine in case someone was bitten by a snake or came down with the dreaded fever, and a large quantity of clothing for the bwana. A machila was prepared. Mr. Dickie would ride in this hammocklike conveyance carried on the shoulders of the men if he got tired of walking.

Deriza Rachel wept when Malinki left her. "I am afraid I will not see you again. And your mother! What will she do if you are killed and she never can see you again?"

"I will come home, *Wokongola*," he replied, using

90

a love name she was fond of. "God will go with me. I am sure of this. He has cared for me in many great perils." He shuddered, remembering the flight from the kraal of the evil Chikunda. He had been very young, but the peril had been so very great that it had been indelibly imprinted on his memory.

Sometimes his mother expressed amazement that he should remember so many things. She was sure that it was because he was something special, a much brighter person than most of the people she knew about. But Malinki did not think it so wonderful that he should remember such events. He knew that he could never forget such momentous occasions. He also knew now that God had a special work for him to do and that God would look after him so long as there was a place in that plan for him to fulfill.

13

On the first day that the party set out to the north-ward to visit the kraal of the Angoni chief, the men killed a large venomous snake, and several times they sighted herds of the lovely impala, gracefully fluid in their running and soaring leaps so that they looked like the running scallops around a Christmas tree. Toward evening of the second day one of the carriers killed one of the lovely creatures. They skinned it and cooked the fresh meat over the fire they had built.

Mr. Dickie had brought a huge bundle of barter material with him. He had beads, cheap bangles, rings, pins, small tin pans, and spoons. Soon after making camp the first evening, the party was sur-rounded by people with small baskets, eggs, fowl, bundles of beans, and bananas. All began speaking at once, trying to agree on terms for barter.

"We'll get some eggs and bananas. We can use them tomorrow!" Mr. Dickie suggested. "We used to fix things to eat ahead when we were back in England. It will save us some time on our journey."

The native carriers looked at each other, puzzled. They were used to hunger and privation. If they had much, they ate much and ate often until all the supplies were gone. If they had nothing, it was accepted with a sort of stoic fatalism. "If it is to be, it is to be, and there is nothing we can do to help it."

But here was a new idea, preparing for the morrow.

Malinki, who had learned to do many things, superintended the boiling of the eggs and packing them and the bananas in a basket.

In the morning the group started early on its journey. As the party went on its way day after day, it often came upon ruined villages. Once they came upon a heap of skeletons and the smoke-blackened remains of a once populous village. "Slavers!" Malinki shuddered, for it was plainly their work.

Malinki remembered dark scenes from his own life. He had known of chiefs selling a man or a woman or a child for a piece of calico or a handful of salt. He knew, too, that all too many chiefs had an absolute disregard for the sacredness of human life, and the farther the group went from Blantyre, the more danger it was in. Slave trade had not been altogether wiped out.

The farther they journeyed up the lake, the more fearful and reluctant the hired porters became. In the evening, after the fires were built and the mattings were laid down for sleeping, Malinki listened to the men who huddled in a group and talked earnestly together.

"We are going to have trouble," he reported to Mr. Dickie. "The carriers are having a *mlandu*. They are talking about something of great importance to them.

They are about to decide something."

"What kind of trouble?" Mr. Dickie asked.

"I think they are going to quit and go back to Blantyre," Malinki said.

And he was right. There was trouble. It took several hours of reasoning and arguing and finally a raise in pay before the carriers would quiet down for the night and agree to go on in the morning.

As they got nearer and yet nearer to the kraal of the big chief, the more fearful the carriers and even Malinki became. Mr. Dickie, who had seen the queen of England on the street of London, could hardly imagine of what they were afraid.

"Why be so scared?" he scoffed. "We have plenty of good gifts for the chief. Why that box of Huntley's biscuits ought to sweeten him up. And then, of course, we have plenty of other good gifts."

Malinki knew it was not so simple as all that. There was real danger. The chief's village was on a high elevation on the western edge of the lake. Tall trees and bush surrounded it and hid it from the view of those approaching it. But the travelers were soon made aware of it. *Impi*, or soldiers of their chief, their splendid muscular bodies clothed in spotted skins of the leopards, challenged their approach. In several places they saw dead bodies in various stages of decay among the deep grasses. Wheeling buzzards glided from the air or took off suddenly as the group approached the spot.

At last the carriers stopped and refused to go one step forward. They were persuaded to stay by the baggage and await the return of Malinki and Mr. Dickie, who would go ahead with a gift for the chief.

94

When the two men got closer to the village, they observed a man crawling on his stomach, very slowly. Every little while as he crawled, he called out loudly a worshipful term. It was a greeting the haughty Angoni chief expected and demanded. The man never looked up as he crawled and shouted. When Malinki and Mr. Dickie reached the chief, Malinki's knees felt like water.

But the visit went better than anyone had hoped. The chief seemed delighted with the tin of biscuits, the long gleaming knife, the tins of jam, and the rolls of different kinds of calico. Mr. Dickie took a can opener and opened a tin of peach jam. The chief stuck his thumb in it and then licked his thumb. He did this over and over, smacking his lips in appreciation. Soon he had eaten the contents of a whole tin. He did take time to bellow an order from his jam-smeared lips, and women began to appear carrying pots of food. There was thick *nsima*, snow-white, made of native ground cornmeal, to be formed into small balls by hand and dipped into the savory *ndiwo* (gravy). There was a pot of speckled beans, cooked with onions and other vegetables that had been cut in chunks. Another dish held cooked greens flavored with crushed peanuts. Everyone ate to his fill while the chief cleaned out another jam tin and ate a quantity of the sweet biscuits that had been neatly packed in a bright-colored tin.

Malinki and Mr. Dickie left the chief's kraal the next day. When they told the carriers about their meeting, the men picked up their burdens cheerfully to start the trek back home. They sang as they jogged along. The loads, as well as their hearts, grew lighter every day. They were going home. They all were alive. Malinki thought of his mother and Deriza Rachel and the trim hut near Chileka village.

And at last Malinki spied Mwasekera and Deriza Rachel a long way off. They had been waiting and watching for him. The meal that night, served on the clean eating mat by his wife's hands, was particularly good, Malinki thought. The sweet potatoes, the nsima, and the bean ndiwo was better than anything he had tasted on the long journey. And even when the villagers gathered to hear the stories and the adventures of his journey, he could not help but feel glad, very glad, to be home. He looked from one dear face to another and thanked God in his heart for His protecting care.

14

Soon after the trip into the interior with Mr. Dickie, Malinki learned that Joseph Booth was going to America and was taking John Chilembwe with him. What would John Chilembwe think of the new country? It was almost fifteen years later that Malinki realized what the trip had done to John.

Joseph Booth said he would see to it that John Chilembwe got an education in America—"because," he declared, "John is deserving of an education. He is aggressive and responsible, and he needs the preparation of a good education to be a real leader of men."

Could it possibly be that this was the cause of John Chilembwe's downfall? Many have thought so. "If he had not been educated, he would not have rebelled," was the way the enemies of Joseph Booth reasoned.

The backers of the mission that had been established by Booth in Nyasaland did not feel that Booth handled the finances properly. They could not possibly know the problems that faced Mr. Booth.

Although a Seventh Day Baptist, Booth had not

talked much about his religious persuasion. He had been more interested in educating the African and lifting his standard of living. Booth had met, when he first landed in Africa, Hettie Hurd (later married to S. N. Haskell) in Cape Town. Sister Hurd was a Seventh-day Adventist. She had tried to persuade Booth to study the Bible truths further, but Booth had not felt it necessary.

When Booth arrived in America, he met Hettie Hurd, now Mrs. Haskell, and her husband once more. They themselves had returned to the States. They invited Booth to their home and took him with them to some meetings held in Chicago. Booth accepted the invitation to tell about his work in central Africa.

Now Booth began to study the beliefs of the Seventh-day Adventist people. Soon he became convinced that he should join the church. He accepted the Adventist's faith. By request of the General Conference committee he went to Battle Creek and gave stirring talks to the Adventists at the sanitarium and in the Tabernacle Church, telling of his experiences in central Africa and inviting the Seventh-day Adventist people to accept the burden of the work in that far-off field. At the close of a Sabbath afternoon meeting the Battle Creek Church in a unanimous vote expressed their approval of the plan to enter mission work in Nyasaland. The people pledged themselves to support Brother Booth in that field for one year.

Since the Seventh Day Baptists wanted to sell the 2001 acres where their mission had been established by Joseph Booth, the Seventh-day Adventists bought the property. Along with Joseph Booth, they sent out a black American family to man the new Adventist mission, Mr. Thomas Branch, his wife, two sons, and daughter Mabel. This family set up housekeeping in one of the brick houses that had been erected by the original owner of the property.

Joseph Booth left America first. It was planned that the Branches would meet him in England. From there they would sail together for Africa.

It was Joseph Booth who told the Branches about Malinki, the man who knew both English and Cinyanja. Booth told Thomas Branch that he had met and worked with Malinki and that he was one of the very few educated natives in the country. He told how Malinki and his friend Golden had gone through the course of study at the Church of Scotland Mission and that Malinki and Golden were the only two Africans in Nyasaland who held teaching certificates.

"Malinki is the man you will need in your work in Nyasaland," Booth said. "He is dependable as well as being qualified. The African Lakes Company have tried everything to get Malinki to work for them full time. He does work for them during the season when school is not in session. He is the only man that has gained the respect of all the carriers for the company. He works as a superintendent and shows a great deal of wisdom in dealing with human nature," Booth went on to extol the virtues of Morrison Malinki.

15

When education in Nyasaland was in its infancy, Malinki, with the help of the villagers and his step-father, before he died, built his own school. It was called, some said, Shiloh Mission, located at Michiru Hill. It was called by some the Sabbath Mission because Malinki taught about the Sabbath in his school. According to Morrison Malinki's own statements, he himself, independent of any other person, found out by reading his Bible the Sabbath truth. He had become the proud possessor of a Bible, translated into the Cinyanja language. Being able to read and lacking any other books in his own language, he naturally turned to the Bible and read it all of his spare time. He made his reading lessons and his writing lessons for his school from the Word of God. He used it for memory work and for copy work. He had seen many books on the shelves in the homes of missionaries, but these were in English or some other European language and were certainly of no use to a teacher of the native people.

Often at night with the sputtering, uncertain light of the small, thick-wicked African lamp, he would read from the Bible to his Deriza Rachel. In due time he came to the twentieth chapter of Exodus. He began to read with great interest the commandments the great God had written on tables of stone and committed to the hands of Moses on a mountain far away called Sinai. He had been taught much of what the commandments said.

Deriza Rachel had learned to enjoy chairs. Malinki had made her one with arms so that she could rest when her day's work was done. Now she sat with their babe in her arms listening to Malinki read from the Book. From time to time Malinki looked up from his reading at the sweet, peaceful face of his wife. He thought of their life together. It was good to have such a wife. It was good that he and Deriza Rachel had been able to tell Kwanona and Mwasekera about the great God who loved all people.

When Malinki read from the Bible in his "preacher voice," Deriza Rachel and Mwasekera would sit proudly and listen. Then he came to the fourth commandment' "*Uzikumbukila tsiku la Sabata likhale lopatulika,*" he read. "*Uzikumbukila tsiku la Sabata likhale lopatulika. Masiku asanulimodz yuzigwira, ndi, kumariza ncio zako zone; koma tsiku lacisanu ndj chiwiri ndilo Sabata.*" Here he had stopped amazed.

"Did you hear that?" he asked in a voice trembling with excitement. "It says here that on the *seventh* day we should worship God in a special way. That is the day that the Europeans call Saturday. I was taught when I was learning Christianity to keep the first day

101

holy—Sunday. Something is wrong here! Someone is wrong, and it cannot be God!" He tapped the page lightly with his fingers.

"No," Deriza Rachel said softly, "No, it cannot be God!"

In the days that followed, Malinki ran everywhere asking, asking, asking, but he got no satisfaction. Some answered one thing and some another. Some said the day was changed when the Lord died on the cross. Some said that the change occurred to make people remember that He was raised from the dead. Malinki read and studied. He finally came to the conclusion that, to be sure, he had better keep both days. As he told Deriza Rachel, "I have heard that God changes not, and He is the same yesterday, today, and forever, and now they tell me He has changed. But I cannot find any place in the Book where it says He has changed."

Then it was that Malinki found out that Booth had returned from America. This was the man who had given him his first real pair of trousers and his first shirt—and his opportunity to teach. He could not help but be grateful to the man. Malinki also learned that Joseph Booth had become a Seventh-day Adventist. Some said he was a turncoat and a religious roustabout. Some of the planters were disgusted with Booth. "Why, the missionaries are bad enough getting the natives all stirred up with piety, but this is ridiculous—keeping Saturday instead of Sunday!" First thing you know the natives will be wanting to lay off work two or three days a week instead of just on Sunday so that they can go to church.

John Chilembwe later came back from America

and he broke with Booth. Chilembwe got possession of a tract of land where he proceeded to build his own church and his own school. At least he did not irritate the other missionaries on that score. But he did on other points. Chilembwe seemed to be a pompous fellow and he sometimes appeared quite ludicrous to those who were searching for faults. His building ventures, inclined to be a little grander than some others of the more modest mission stations, were jeered at. His long-tailed coats, his striped pants, his fine hats, his wife's taffeta dresses all brought forth criticism from both the whites and the blacks.

Malinki also came in for criticism when he began to keep the Sabbath, though he did it most inostensibly. Nevertheless, he soon became known for his Sabbath keeping, and he was severely criticized for it by those whom he had known and admired at other places. But so strong was his belief that he was doing the will of God that he went right on and did not change.

But talk against Booth was violent. "He came here a Baptist. Then he got interested in the Church of Christ for a while. Then, of all things, it was the Russellites, or they call themselves 'Millennial Dawns.' Then he got himself mixed up with the Seventh Day Baptists. Now, would you believe it, we hear he is in trouble with them over finances, and he has offered his services to the Seventh-day Adventists. He may become a Moslem next the way he is going." These were some of the criticisms voiced against Booth.

Malinki listened to the talk without commenting himself. But he studied on in the Bible. Which day was right? The problem could be solved only by prayer and by study of the Holy Bible.

One day while going home from Blantyre, Malinki in deep thought walked along on hard red paths past scraggly bushes and trees. Occasionally a monkey or a baboon leaped into trees near him and chittered or yapped angrily. Once he passed by a loaded *msuku* tree and got a pocketful of the small round nuts. These he ate after splitting the tough husks with his thumbnail. He passed men, women, and children, but he hardly stopped to greet them, for he was thinking so deeply. He had been keeping two *Sabatas*, and of course people thought it strange; and the planters protested angrily that he did not know his own mind. "Which day is right?" The thought kept racing through his mind. "I will have to keep both days until I know for sure," he decided humbly, for he honestly wanted to do what the great God wanted him to do.

He got to his neat home where Deriza Rachel had the pots of *nsima* and *ndiwo* ready and waiting. She had a pot of cool clean water too in which to soak his tired, hot, dusty feet. After the evening meal he would study more this puzzling question.

16

At school he explained his two rest days to his bright-faced students. "Now we must do all of our work in five days," he explained. "We will have to do six days' work in five until I find out which is the right day. I know God will help me," he added. Then with great solemnity he read the Ten Commandments to his wide-eyed pupils of all ages. There were children who wanted to learn to read and write, and grandpas and grandmas, men, and women with babes tied to their backs crowded into the primer classes. They were all eager to master this strange thing called reading. "We will commit to memory the Ten Commandments," Malinki told his class. And every day the chorus of voices repeated over and over the ten laws of God made for the happiness of men. The more Malinki heard it repeated, the more convinced he was in the truth of the seventh-day Sabbath.

He had been advised by his former friends to read more in *Cipangano Catsopano* (the New Testament). He was told by his old teachers in Blantyre that the

New Testament was more for people today than the Old Testament, which was really nothing but an old history of the Jews. But when Malinki took to reading extensively in the New Testament, he found to his surprise that Jesus Himself kept the Sabbath. He also read in the fifth chapter of Matthew that not even the smallest part of the law would pass away. Heaven and earth would pass before such a thing would occur! These were strong words, and they convinced Malinki. His whole school then began to keep one day, and that was the seventh, just as the commandment had adjured him.

Then an amazing thing happened. Padding up the path to his home and school one day came a donkey with a kindly faced man riding on its back. Malinki went out to meet the man. He was black, but was not the same kind of person Malinki met in his everyday life. It was plain to be seen that this man was different. He wore the clothes of an *Azungu* with the ease that showed Malinki that wearing the white man's clothes had always been his custom. He was a tall man, with an open, intelligent countenance.

After greeting him Malinki invited him to sit on the bench he had made in front of his house.

"I am Thomas Branch," the man said. "I have come to the mission that has recently been bought by the Seventh-day Adventists. The people around call the mission the Malamulo Mission because we keep God's law. I have heard about you, Mr. Malinki, several times," he went on. "But when I learned that you keep the seventh-day Sabbath, I knew you were the man for our mission. We have been praying for a man who knows English and who has a good character. You fit in very well. You can be of inestimable help."

Then he told Malinki and Deriza Rachel, who had come out of the house, of his wife and children. "My daughter, Mabel, is working to organize our school, and we have the beginnings of a hospital. We have built a church house and will use it also for a school until we can build a separate building. We need you, Mr. Malinki. We hope you will come to us as soon as you complete your school term here."

"I'll consider it," Malinki said. Then he and Deriza Rachel talked it over and decided they should go.

"It would be wonderful to be in a place where everyone is a Christian, and where everyone keeps the Sabbath," Malinki said, turning to Thomas Branch. "I will have to have more knowledge of the truths of God's Word," he said wistfully. Here was a man who must really know the Bible, and who would be able to help him to understand, Malinki felt sure. They sat for a long time that evening by the flickering lamp while Thomas Branch opened up more truths than Malinki had ever dreamed existed. He learned of the imminent coming of the Lord and of the fast-fulfilling signs which show the Word of God is true. He also learned that Christians do not eat as others do. "Christians do not adorn themselves with expensive or even cheap trinkets, but with the adorning of a meek and a quiet spirit. None of the bangles, rings, bracelets, nose rings, earrings, and nose jewels are for Christians who are looking for the soon coming of the Lord," Mr. Branch said.

Malinki looked over at Deriza Rachel while this new friend was talking. He smiled as he saw her quietly removing the few cheap ornaments she possessed.

Mr. Branch knew very little about the Cinyanja language, and he expressed pleasure that Malinki could handle English so well. "My daughter is trying to get a hymn book together, but no one on the mission has a good enough knowledge of both languages to be of much help. I am sure you can help us in this chore."

Malinki and Deriza Rachel gladly consented to move to the new mission as soon as the school term was over. The next day she began to pack up the few possessions she had, getting ready for this move. But before the school term ended and time for the move came, Mwasekera was laid to rest in the little cemetery beside Kwanona. Both of them had become firm believers in the Christian religion before they died. This was a comfort to Malinki.

Mr. Branch sent several strong mission boys to help the Malinki family move. An oxcart made the moving lighter. The few possessions were piled into it, and the oxen plodded slowly down the road.

When the family arrived at Malamulo Mission, they were instructed to go to the Branch home first. Malinki marveled to see the fine brick house that the Branches lived in. It reminded him of Mandala House. Mandala House had two stories and much more room, but this was a most pleasant house, which the German settler had built years before.

"Come in! Come in!" Thomas Branch opened the door wide to the travelers. Mrs. Branch whisked Deriza Rachel and little James to a washroom where they could wash in a big bowl that had pictures of flowers on the side and a jug or a pitcher to match. Deriza Rachel looked about her. What she saw made her eyes open wide. She would have her husband build her such a room for washing alone, she decided. There were several long white pieces of cloth that Mrs. Branch called towels. Soap was kept in a small dish with flowers on it too. Mrs. Branch gave her a small square of cloth similar to the towels. "This is a washcloth," she said. "You use it to wash with." She showed Deriza Rachel how to wash James's face with the little square washcloth. Then she went back into what Mrs. Branch called the parlor, and Mr. Branch took Malinki for his turn in the washroom.

Deriza Rachel marveled at a certain kind of chair that was in this parlor. Under the legs were long, curved pieces of wood. When she sat down in the chair she was sure it was going to turn over with her, but it simply had a swaying motion that was pleasant when you got used to it—back and forth, back and forth. Deriza Rachel noticed that Mrs. Branch seemed to like swaying back and forth and did not seem to be in the least alarmed for fear she would go over onto the floor. There were soft things on the chairs, unbelievably soft, which were called cushions or pillows. There was an amazing heavy strong cloth on the floor, which had pictures of flowers and leaves. It seemed a shame to walk upon it, but Mrs. Branch did so, and so did Mr. Branch. There were pictures on the walls, pictures of trees and houses. The red cement floor of the porch and the rooms in the house shone, as a result of waxing them with Stoep Wax and Polish, she learned.

A table stood in the middle of the room, while off to one side against the wall were shelves. And there were many books on the shelves. How could one man own so many? Deriza Rachel saw Malinki's eyes beam when he looked at all the books. She hoped Bwana Branch would let Malinki borrow them one at a time so that he could read them and gain much knowledge.

Two kitchen boys helped Mrs. Branch in the kitchen. One was the cook and the other, a helper called the *tsukumbali* (plate washer). Both came in quietly now and put a white cloth on the big table in the eating room. From some other shelves they took the most beautiful dishes that Deriza Rachel had ever seen. There were shining utensils the Malinkis learned were knives, forks, and spoons. These were laid beside the plates.

Then they all gathered about this table and enjoyed the most wonderful meal the Malinki family had ever eaten. Delicious! Delectable! More than good! They smacked their lips in appreciation.

The Branch family spread a yellow grease on pieces of food called *mkăté* (bread). Malinki had seen some in Mandala House at one time when he was there near mealtime. He had told Deriza Rachel that the *Azungu* like *mkăté* very much. Little James Malinki ate several slices, for Mrs. Branch brought out something called jam to spread on it.

"*Amai*," he said to his mother, "this is the best thing I have tasted."

It is made of guavas and Cape gooseberries," Mrs. Branch told Deriza Rachel. "I will show you how to make it when you get settled."

Deriza Rachel puzzled over the white potatoes that had been fixed in a most marvelous way. They looked like nothing so much as some of the great white billowing clouds one sees so often in the sky.

Mrs. Branch explained that they were mashed. "I put butter, salt, milk or cream in them after they are cooked. Then I mash them with a masher and beat them smooth and fluffy."

There was so much to wonder at—the gravy, the dumplings with the beans, the candied sweet potatoes.

"I cannot eat more," Malinki said, patting his full stomach. "No, I could not eat another bite."

The cook and the *tsukumbali* came in and took away the plates. Then the cook brought in a strange three-cornered piece of something on a smaller plate. There seemed to be two layers, or a lid on top of some fruit with a lid on the bottom. Mrs. Branch told them it was Cape gooseberry pie.

Although Malinki had said he couldn't eat another bite, somehow he managed to clean his plate.

Deriza Rachel sighed when she tasted the pie. "Never will I be able to make food taste as this does!" she said, looking at Mrs. Branch.

After dinner Malinki and Deriza Rachel went to see their new home, which was near the church and the new dispensary. It was beyond their expectation, a pleasant house with two rooms and an outside kitchen. There was a porch, called a *khonde*, all the way around the house. It had a door that closed. Wonderful things called hinges helped the door to be opened and closed easily without its dragging on the floor. There was glass in the windows so that standing on the inside one could actually see outside. Malinki and Deriza Rachel could hardly imagine this was to be their home.

And so began the new life of this family starting in the work of the Lord for the Seventh-day Adventist Church. And it was to go on for many, many years. Malinki lived past the century mark, and worked for the Lord to the very end. And, to the very end he had utmost faith in the coming of the Lord. He became known throughout the area as a man of God. And his sons have followed in their father's steps.

17

But what of John Chilembwe? John Chilembwe, at his own mission, dressed as he had seen those in America dress. He wore shirts, pants, coats, shoes, and neckties. He tried desperately to achieve a certain dignity and social standing for himself. He had ambitions to see his people in Africa do as he had seen his race doing in America. They wore clothes, had employment, lived in houses, and took care of their own. The houses he had seen in America, even the poor ones, were better than the mud huts and the kraals many of his people lived in here in Africa. His African brothers in America slept in beds and cooked food on stoves. He wanted his people to have all the advantages the blacks in America had. He had little concept of the struggle that had gone on in America, the struggle for a certain amount of freedom for the blacks. Chilembwe did not take into account that the blacks of America had had two centuries of rubbing shoulders with this so-called civilization. His people did not have a tenth of that.

113

The blacks in America had harnessed horses, shod them, made harnesses. Some of them had been apprenticed to carriage makers. They had seen much machinery and easier ways of doing necessary things. Lumber was cut by steam power, not by the blistering agonizing manpower that was all Africa knew. True, European countries had brought in the railroad, and its iron rails were slowly penetrating to the darkest parts of the continent. But these things were a matter of course in America. The shrieking, rumbling trains carried cargoes that would have broken the heads and backs of the carriers.

Grimly, but courageously, Chilembwe endeavored to override the taboos of his people and to get them to develop a higher standard of living. Many of them feared and opposed progress such as this. Some of them did not like to wear coats, shoes, and long sleeves in the sweltering heat. John and his wife liked to dress fully. They seemed to feel this was the road to equality with their brothers of America; they followed the best way they could.

Both Morrison Malinki and John Chilembwe wanted something better for their own people. Malinki found Christ to be the answer to the problem. Malinki brought Christ to his people. John Chilembwe tried force and coercion. His name has gone down in the history of his country, not as a savior but as a rebel.

Thwarted again and again in his plans, Chilembwe allowed rancor to grow and soon he was ready to reach for weapons. It must be said, and it is believed, at first his motives to help his people were good. If he felt the urge of his personal ability to lead his people to a higher plane of existence, surely that is pardonable. Certainly, the cold fury at being frustrated unjustly again and again, if one looks at the overall picture, could be counted as purely human. Yet it did not stop there. No rebellious outbreak can be kept within bounds when a mob is aroused. The festering epidemic of hate began to spread, and it was not altogether his fault.

One night Malinki, now the pastor at the Malamulo Mission, and his little family were asleep on their mats in their home when a knocking sound came on their glass window and someone called in a whisper, "Sst—Sst. *Odi, odi.*"

It had rained in the night, and at first when Malinki and Deriza Rachel awoke they thought it was the wind shaking the wooden shutters. Malinki got up and opened the door and peered out. Two men stood in the shadows on his *khonde.*

"Do not make a light. What we say can well be understood in the dark," said a low voice that Malinki instantly recognized to be the voice of his friend of former years, John Chilembwe.

Malinki stepped out onto the *khonde.* The two men sat down in chairs and began to talk. At first Malinki listened eagerly, for was not this man with Chilembwe a fine, clean, clever man? Had he not spent many years being educated in America to be a doctor?

They recounted to Malinki many grievances, many of them actual and recognized. They urged Malinki to join them in ridding the country of the hated white man. They recounted the injustices, humiliations, and cruelties, which in many cases were all too true.

"It is unbearable, and we cannot, will not, stand it much longer," Chilembwe said hotly, pounding one

115

clenched fist into the palm of his other hand. "No, we who are educated and who want to get ahead are hindered on every side. They do not want us out of the rut of servitude. There is no hope for progress as long as they are here. I say 'Africa for Africans.' " He said this so vehemently, that Malinki felt Deriza Rachel, who had come to stand by him, tremble.

Could it be that this sweet reign of peace at the mission was going to come to an end? Malinki felt puzzled and sad. He looked at his wife and then at John Chilembwe and the other man. Could it be there was not going to be peace but instead struggle and bloodshed and perhaps—yes perhaps—slavery again?

The man with Chilembwe, Dr. John Gray Kufa, did not talk as much as Chilembwe. When he did speak, it was with great conviction. He told Malinki that as a medical attendant at the Magomera Estates, he was brought face-to-face again and again with flagrant injustices. "The white men do not care for lives unless they are their own," he said softly. "They have great soft beds in their houses while our sick and dying are on mats on the hard ground. It is our people who are making the riches for them. Our people are plowing, reaping, picking tea and coffee for them—and at such miserable wages. We could not live if we did not raise all our food in our gardens. This is not right."

This talk went on and on, much of it true, of grievances hard to be borne at the hands of ruthless, unprincipled men. "Surely, surely, the good David Livingstone had not opened Africa for it to be a prey to such a swarm of locusts!" Malinki thought. Suddenly a cold fear filled him. Here were men who were so desperate that they were willing to fight, even against the government. In his heart he knew this was all wrong. Two wrongs never make a right.

John Chilembwe went on, "Now, Malinki, we need you. You are a leader, you are clever, you are educated. You have a following. We have everything planned. Our plans have been laid with great care. We will get first the rascal of a man who is related to the great Dr. Livingstone. The rascal goes out of his way to make trouble for us. How the good man, Dr. Livingstone, had such kin is hard to understand. We plan also to march on Top Mandala and Zomba. Arms and ammunition we know are stored at Top Mandala.

"But, John," protested Malinki, "not all white men are bad. A white man helped you to be all you are. Suppose Mr. Booth had not helped you? He was a good man, no matter what people say. If the men of the Church of Scotland had not helped me—if good Dr. Livingstone had not come to Africa—why, John, you and I would be back in the bush villages, sharpening spears and living as our fathers did for thousands of years. John, you know we ought to live meaningful lives, help our people—."

But John Chilembwe, his eyes stony, and flashing with hate interrupted the gentle pleading of Malinki, "I have broken with Booth," he said sharply, incisively, as a knife thrust. "He, as you know, hardly knows his own mind. While I do honor him and respect him in my heart, I know he won't win. He is so peace-loving that he will hardly kill a mosquito. He will let these buzzards destroy him, Malinki. I won't. I will fight, and I will win." Again he brought a clenched fist down hard into the palm of his other hand.

"But, John, I have been brought up in the midst of

tears, bloodshed, slavery, beating, starvation, horror, fire. Surely, John, you—you—are a Christian. Did you not read, 'Love your enemies'? Doesn't Christ mean more to you than this?" Malinki was aghast at the resentment, the hate and revenge, the malignancy these two men harbored. "This thing is like a great coiled serpent, all-encompassing, with fangs out, ready to poison—to kill, kill, kill," Malinki spoke quietly. "And this from men who have received great benefits from the race you are planning to destroy? And all because of a few unjust and unprincipled men?"

The two men stared at Malinki.

"Both of you, like me, have received much good from white men," Malinki went on. "There are good and bad in all races, John. The Arabs and the Portuguese would still be at our throats if it were not for the English. My mother—"

But Chilembwe interrupted harshly. "This is not the time for peaceful testimonials," he sneered and beat the table so hard in his irritation that Deriza Rachel drew back behind Malinki. "Too much has happened. We cannot, we will not, bear anymore of this impertinence. There are hundreds of strong men who are waiting with spears and bows and arrows to wipe Africa clean of these men. Now tell me, Yes or No, are you with your own people, or are you with the enemy?"

"I do not have a Yes or a No to this, John. I cannot be on your side or against my people if I follow the Lord. You know I have done nothing since I have obtained my education but try to help my people. I am working here with good people. This mission keeps the *malamulo*, all ten of them. And one of them says, and you know it, 'Thou shalt not kill'!"

John bent forward, his face intense, his eyes gleaming like those of an angry beast. "It is not murder to kill these men who oppress us. Even in the Bible God told Joshua to destroy some people from off the face of the earth. If a few good people have to be killed with the many evil ones, that we cannot help. We will have Africa for Africans!" He spoke with studied venom. "You may have to be taken care of if you champion the cause of our enemies." The two men rose to leave.

The two figures melted away, leaving a throbbing darkness. It was as if the beast, Hate, was still there, audibly breathing out venom and violence.

Malinki never saw John Chilembwe again. Nor did he hear from the man, John Gray Kufa. If circumstances had been as God would have had them, how much good both of them could have done for their people! Hate and violence, injustice and reprisal, ultimately destroyed them both and for a long time put a great cloud over further development for the African people.

For many days the Malinki household had little rest or sleep. Something strange seemed to fill the very air. Unrest seemed to possess everyone. The feeling of impending disaster filtered through from village to village. Knots of students would gather and talk worriedly. Something terrible seemed to be hovering ready to strike. The men of the villages sat in close circles mumbling and shaking their heads. The women went about their work but with furtive glances and much trembling.

Malinki felt constrained to go to the brick house and tell the mission director of the night visitors and of the threats.

When he heard the story, the director placed a hand on Malinki's shoulder and said, "'If God be for us, who can be against us?' Here at Malamulo we do not participate in violence. Our work is to teach Christ and Christ only." After a pause he added, "We will put several extra night watchmen on duty to patrol the small compound for a while. That may help to ease the tension."

18

William Jervis Livingstone, a kin of the good Dr. Livingstone, was not a missionary but a fortune hunter. He had had, it was said, several superstitious prognostications made regarding him, some even in Scotland, where he was born. Rumor had it that when Livingstone's wedding occurred, a guest died when the shafts of the vehicle in which he rode to the wedding broke and he was hurled backward, his head hitting against a stone. The old ones, inured to generations of omens, tokens, and evil signs, shook their wise, grizzled heads, "Some evil will come to this man," they said sagely, "if even the angel of death visits his wedding."

The talk went on: "If the pale, scythed horseman was already pacing by the side of William Jervis— well—. And you know very well he was never very patient or tolerant. He is greedy and selfish; that goes against him." This was the man Chilembwe had reported would be the first victim.

The news came to Malamulo. It came remarkably

quick for those days of word of mouth or throbbing drums. The day dawned sunny and warm as usual. Monkeys leaped in the trees and the baboons yapped; women pounded mealies and chattered as they worked; babies cried. Village life was going on as it had for generations. The news came that Chilembwe had killed William Jervis Livingstone and Duncan MacCormick. Something of the old savagery had apparently come into John Chilembwe and his men. In the church that Chilembwe had built with so much sweat and tears, on Sunday during the sermon the congregation sat stunned as the dripping heads of Livingstone and MacCormick were placed on the altar.

And now men without a conscience marched beside lawmen and even avowed Christians. One could not tell who was for and who was against the rebels. Chilembwe's church, which had been rather a wonderful piece of architecture built by a man of his background and culture, was destroyed. It had cost so much to build, and it seemed to be the culmination of so many dreams and ambitions. Through the rubble of the destroyed church the crocheted edges of an altar cloth protruded.

Word of mouth said that John Chilembwe and John Gray Kufa were shot down. Where they were buried no one knows. Some say they both escaped and both of them got to America and lived out their lives in comparative peace under changed names. Later a man who came to the hospital at Malamulo Mission declared that he was the one who had fired the shot that had killed John Chilembwe. So the rumors went. Someday, when the judgment is set and the books are opened, the Judge of all the earth will weigh men in His just balances. Morrison Malinki, John Chilembwe, and William Jervis Livingstone will all receive their rewards, for He knows what is in men's hearts.

Many of the rebels were caught attempting to get at the store of guns at Top Mandala. Then, perhaps for revenge, or simply because of jealousy, Malinki's name was mentioned as an accomplice. This was, many think, an instruction given by John Chilembwe himself because Malinki would not join in the plot. Gentle, peace-loving Morrison Malinki was to be punished.

All at Malamulo were horrified when soldiers marched in and put their gentle, kindly pastor in irons and roughly marched him away. Malinki dimly thought that he was glad Mwasekera was not alive to see this terrible day. He heard poor Deriza Rachel scream and then saw her faint. Their gentle, manly young son, James, looked on in horror. Even the protests of the mission director were of no avail. The whole mission wept and wailed to see him clamped in irons and roughly thrust down the red-soiled road.

At the mission entrance Malinki looked back. Would he ever see this lovely place again? Would he have to die because of the accusations of his false friend? A prayer escaped his lips, "Oh, Father, forgive them."

It was a motley, wretched assortment of human beings that were marched in clanking irons the many weary miles to Zomba, the government headquarters. At that time a man was guilty until his innocence was proved. Whips, the dreaded *chikoti*, sang often and plucked bits of flesh from the bare backs of the plodding prisoners if they fell behind in the brisk march

123

under the boiling sun. Dust enveloped the prisoners in thick clouds. Thirst became almost unbearable. Many of the men cursed and wished for death.

But Malinki plodded along uncomplaining; he did not accuse or speak to anyone. Sometimes he sang, and sometimes he repeated over and over precious promises he had learned from the Good Book.

Some of the songs he sang were those he had helped Mabel Branch to translate from the English for the Nyanja hymnal. One of his favorites was:

Pakuitana Mbuye Wanga,
Potsiriza dzikoli
Pa kufika tsikula kuwalalo
Posangkhana akumvera
A kuona Yesuyo
Tidzakondwerera pomkomanaye.

Mabel had told him that in America this song was entitled "When the Roll Is Called Up Yonder." Malinki did not doubt that unless God intervened, he would have to lay down his life with those who were really guilty. His name had been given as one of those who had planned the slaughter. Besides, he was an educated African, and he kept the Sabbath. It all added up. It was as simple as that.

Enemies pointed out that it had been shown again and again that the educated got a little too ambitious, impertinent, and demanding; they were never so subservient to shouted commands as before. Malinki was educated. He must be guilty.

On the grueling hard march in clanking irons to Zomba, Malinki thought of men in the Dark Ages the mission director and Pastor Branch had told of in sermons—of good men and women who had died in their innocence. They were called martyrs. Perhaps he would be a martyr. He remembered that the pastor had said that they had counted it joy to be able to die for the Lord Jesus and all the goodness and kindness He stood for. He took comfort in thinking of these things. He did not shout, mutter menacingly, or stand with sullen hate gleaming from his eyes as many did who were in this company. He was one apart, and the peace of Jesus Christ sat upon him until his captors could not help but sense it. Though the shadow of death, though the hangman's noose hung above him, like Paul and Silas he sang in his prison cell. Once he asked humbly for a Bible, but it was refused him.

He was straightforward and frank in his testimonies. He showed that though he, with others, had been associated for an extremely short time with John Chilembwe, when he had come out of the Church of Scotland Mission with his hand-written teacher's certificate, it had been many years since he had had any direct dealings with John Chilembwe. He had been with the Malamulo Mission since 1904. When Dr. Kufa and John Chilembwe had come to his hut, he had labored to dissuade them when he was urged to join them. He had been threatened with reprisal. This accusation was their revenge.

The Malamulo Mission director at the time, Elder Robinson, went to Zomba to add his voice attesting to Malinki's innocence. It was not for Malinki alone he was pleading; it was for the cause of all Christian missions in all that part of Africa.

Ruthless men, goaded on by frustrated desires to exploit all, stoutly asserted and many believed that missions and schools were the cause of all this trouble.

The planters, the miners, and many of the European settlers were for the closing of all the missions and schools and sending the missionaries home, troublemakers that they were.

Men searching for cheap labor in the mines did not want an educated African. An educated one would not be satisfied with the small wages, cheap brass baubles, sleazy cheap cloth, and rotten beer.

Back at Malamulo Mission many prayers ascended to God for Malinki's life. Good men of every faith interviewed officials with data and with records and pleaded the cause of Christianity in Malinki's behalf. The Church of Scotland officials had nothing but good to say of Malinki, except that he had probably been duped into accepting some things believed by Joseph Booth.

Nothing evil was proved, and at last Malinki was allowed to go free. The thing that had saved him was his good, exemplary life. Had he been militant in the least, he would have been hanged with the rest.

And now the real Christians all over central Africa breathed easier. There were many missions started, as David Livingstone had dreamed, to train men and women to make a better Africa. Livingstonia Mission stood like a rampart to the north. There were the Church of Scotland, the Church of England, and Malamulo Mission.

Many years later when Malamulo Mission celebrated its fiftieth anniversary, Morrison Malinki's voice quavered as he sang for more than a thousand gathered for Sabbath School that morning of April 26, 1952.

Pakuitana Mbuye Wanga,
Potsiriza dsikoli

Pa kufika tsikula kuwalalo
Posangkhana akumvera
A kuona Yesuyo
Tidzakondwerera pomkomanaye.

His voice grew stonger as he sang the lines, "When the roll is called up yonder, I'll be there."

Pastor Morrison Malinki, who was then almost 100 years old, the first native teacher, whose jet-black hair had grown white in years of service, told of those early days and of his continued confidence and hope in the God he had learned to trust.

Out there in old Nyasaland, now called Malawi, is a grave with a small marker at its head. A grave showing the resting place of one Morrison Malinki, age approximately 109 years. He and Deriza Rachel await the coming of the Lifegiver. Deriza Rachel was laid to rest at approximately 106 years of age. Up to the end her mind was keen and clear, and although bent almost double, she walked to Sabbath School every Sabbath morning until the end of her life in the '70s.

But what about John Chilembwe? Where is his grave? He is gone. His followers are all but forgotten.

All over Malinki's Africa are schools, churches, hospitals, and printing plants giving the message that Jesus is coming again. He will make all wrongs right. He is the African's God, the God of all people.

Two of Malinki's sons, James and Joseph, have both given many years of service to the cause their father held dear. Both are ordained ministers. James went as one of our first African missionaries to Zaire. Later he worked in Zambia. James had a wonderful gift for languages and dialects. After 56 years of active ser-

vice he has retired. Joseph still lives near the Malamulo Mission and Blantyre where his father first
learned of the God of heaven who knows no racial
barriers but has love for everyone.

Nyasaland is now Malawi. Educated Africans sit
on the council. Missions have sprung up the length
and breadth of the country. Malamulo Mission now
has a college. There is a large leper colony there also
where many hundreds of lepers have seen the horrible
symptoms arrested. More important, they have found
a cure for the leprosy of sin. They have gone home to
their families and villages to live a life that is exemplary to their people. Mombera, once the seat of the
warlike Angoni tribe, now has a thriving school and
dispensary. In this small lake country where 100 years
ago slave trade caused so much misery and degradation, now there are over 34,000 members who are
willing emissaries of Jesus Christ, thanks to such men
as David Livingstone, Thomas Branch, Morrison Malinki, and all those who have followed on.